TEMPT ME

Bodyguard Bad Boys

NEW YORK TIMES BESTSELLING AUTHOR

CARLY PHILLIPS

Copyright © Karen Drogin 2017
Print Edition
CP Publishing 2017
Cover Design: Letitia Hasser, RBA Designs
Cover Photography: Sara Eirew Photography
Formatting: BB eBooks

Bodyguard Bad Boys… Sexy, hot and oh so protective!

Burned by an ex with a wandering eye, Austin Rhodes has sworn off women. His sole focus is his young daughter – and despite his good intentions, the little girl's live-in nanny. He hired Mia Atwood to care for his child but he finds himself lusting after her instead. Keeping his distance isn't easy but he's determined to be a gentleman. Until Mia's past comes back to haunt her and she's in need of Austin's brand of protection. Suddenly she's his in every sense of the word—and he'll do whatever it takes to shield the woman who tempts him beyond reason.

* * *

Chapter One

THE AFTERNOON SUN shone through the windows in the warm, cozy kitchen. Mia Atwood held Bailey Rhodes' little fingertips in one hand and carefully painted the six-year-old's nails, trying her best to keep the color off the child's skin. "So tomorrow you start first grade. Are you ready?" she asked her small charge.

Bailey looked up at her with her father's big brown eyes. "I'm 'cited. Lisa's in my class but Callie isn't." She pouted as she reminded herself of that fact. "And Lisa said Josh Rockman is with us." She wrinkled her small nose. "Eew. He's gross so I hope he isn't sitting near me, but his last name starts with an R, too. So maybe he is. He used to be at the table across from me in Ms. Diamond's class," the little chatterbox said.

Mia bit the inside of her cheek to keep from laughing. "I'm sure Josh isn't gross, Bailey."

"He's a *boy*," Bailey said, drawing out the word

with a negative tone, as if that fact explained everything.

Mia waved her hand over the polish, hoping to
help it dry before Bailey was off to play and smudged
Mia's work. "All finished but can you sit for a few
minutes so it dries?"

"Yeah." Bailey held up her hands and grinned, a
nearly toothless smile because she'd lost her front
teeth and they'd only just begun to grow in. So. Cute.
"Can I watch TV?" she asked.

"I have to get dinner ready, so I'll put it on in the
family room." Mia gestured to the room across from
the kitchen with a completely open view of the sofa
and television from where Mia would prepare the
evening meal.

"Wait. I'll put some oil on your nails to help them
set." She applied the oil, then led Bailey to the sofa in
the family room. "How about you keep your hands
right here?" Mia placed them palms down on Bailey's
thighs, turned on her favorite show, and hoped it kept
her occupied while the polish dried.

For the last three months, she'd been a live-in
nanny for Bailey, hired by the child's single father,
Austin Rhodes. He lived in Connecticut, wanting his
daughter to grow up in the suburbs, in a house with
neighbors and a backyard in which to play. There was
no Mrs. Rhodes in the picture. Her employer hadn't

explained except to say he had sole custody… and Mia hadn't asked questions.

She had enough in her own work background he hadn't pushed hard about when hiring her. Her last job hadn't been a cakewalk. Her employer had been into shady dealings and she'd heard too much, learned things she'd had to report to the authorities and testify about at trial.

Austin had only cared that she'd stepped up and done the right thing in the courts, and he'd had no problem hiring her. He didn't care about the details. Of course, she wasn't stupid. He was a bodyguard with access to all sorts of information, so he'd probably found out the particulars on his own. As for the elusive one-time Mrs. Rhodes, Bailey never mentioned her mom, either, but when it came to Austin, Mia couldn't help but wonder why any woman would let him go.

Not going there, she reminded herself before her thoughts could drift to the man who kept himself in shape courtesy of a downstairs gym and who had well-defined muscles and sexy tattoos. He also possessed a chiseled face with a strong chin and full lips, jet-black hair, longer on top, and a constant, sexy scruff of a beard. And before she let herself linger on him any longer—she was only human, after all—she pushed her wayward thoughts away.

He had no place in her mind. During her work as a nanny, she'd come into contact with men who thought she was available for extracurricular activities as well as child care, something that both offended and upset her. These men were married, for one thing, and she never wanted to be that cliché, the nanny who had an affair with her wealthy employer. Even if, in this case, he was single. Thank goodness Austin wasn't one of those men. He'd always treated her with distant kindness and respect.

"Mia, I messed a nail," Bailey called out, interrupting her thoughts long before Mia had even started prepping dinner.

She shook her head and laughed. "Come on over and I'll fix it."

Before Bailey could make her way back to the kitchen, the state-of-the-art alarm system beeped, alerting Mia to the fact that Austin—he insisted she call him by his first name or else he'd think she was talking about his father—was home.

He walked in through the garage side door as he did every evening he didn't have an assignment that kept him out odd hours.

"Daddy!" Bailey squealed and ran to her father, who scooped her up before she could barrel into him.

"What's up, Bailey Button?" he asked, using his nickname for his daughter.

She giggled as she always did. "Mia did my nails. See?" She shoved her hand in his face, too close for him to get a good look.

He pulled her wrist farther away and studied her purple nails as if they were the most important thing in the world to him, and Mia's heart melted.

"Gorgeous!" he exclaimed, with more feeling than she'd have thought the man could muster over a manicure.

In the short time she'd been here, she'd seen firsthand that he was an amazing father and Bailey was a lucky girl. Having grown up in foster care, Mia knew how special the father-daughter bond was—or rather, she knew how much she'd missed in not having it. Her father had walked out on her and her mother when she was two, so she barely remembered him. She'd lost her mom a few years later to cancer, so she knew how fortunate the little girl was to have a dad like Austin.

"I messed one up so Mia has to fix it," the little girl said, wriggling out of her father's embrace.

"Come on, munchkin," Mia called out to her. "Let's fix you. Then I need to get dinner prepped."

"I'm going to exercise first, so don't rush," Austin said.

Mia nodded. "No worries. It's a stir-fry, so I'll get everything ready and I won't start until you're finished showering," she said, aware of his routine.

"Thanks."

She busied herself with Bailey's nails and not with thinking about a sweaty Austin working out in his downstairs gym, the muscles flexing as he moved, or his hot body in the shower afterwards. She was the nanny and that's all she'd ever be.

★ ★ ★

AUSTIN HAD A long day. He wouldn't call the situation he'd been in a hostage crisis but it had been damned close. Too close for a man with a child at home, that was for sure.

The woman he'd been guarding had snuck out to meet with her ex while Austin had been busy with her little girl. He usually received the kid-friendly jobs because, according to his boss, Dan Wilson, Austin was good with children. As if having his own made him an expert on other people's kids. Being around other kids only made him long for his daughter because at least he understood her... until the teenage years hit. He shuddered at the thought.

After a long, hard workout, weights and cardio included, he stepped into a hot shower and let the steam relax his muscles. As he washed up and shampooed his hair, his stomach growled, reminding him it was time for dinner. Which, of course, reminded him of his daughter's nanny, whose blonde hair was usually in a messy bun looking sexy when she wasn't intending it to be. At the thought of her, his body came to life, and it took all his willpower not to jerk off to the thought of her.

He was beyond lucky he'd found his Mia through a reputable service and she had amazing cooking skills. Add in that Bailey seemed to adore her and he couldn't mess up a good thing by coming on to the nanny.

Before Mia, his parents had been Bailey's caregivers and although John and Sarah were young and spry, it hadn't been fair to expect them to give up their lives to take care of Austin's child. No matter that they loved their granddaughter, they'd already raised their kids, Austin and his sister, Sharon.

Head on straight, he dried himself off and pulled on a pair of black track pants and a light blue tee shirt, then headed downstairs to find his daughter.

As he approached the kitchen, Bailey's chatter reached his ears.

"Mia, would you come with Daddy to bring me to school?"

The sound of stir-fry sizzling in the wok acted as stereo to Mia's reply. "Your daddy is excited to take you tomorrow. He even took off from work so he could be there. You don't want to disappoint him, do you?"

"No, but…" Bailey hesitated. "Everyone's going to have their mommies and I won't and I'll be sad. So can you come, please? I know you're not my mommy but you're a girl. So pretty please, come take me?"

His daughter's words were like a punch in the gut. Austin hadn't left Kayla, she'd walked out on him and their daughter, not once but twice. True, he'd married her because she was pregnant, on purpose, she'd admitted, but he'd been determined to make the marriage work. Unfortunately, not only had she been a shitty wife, she'd been a worse mother, and that was where Austin drew the line. Anything that hurt his daughter was unacceptable.

He shook his head, determined to stay in the present with the one person who mattered. "Hey, guys, something smells good!" He joined Bailey and Mia in the kitchen, where Mia was placing servings of delicious-looking stir-fried chicken and vegetables on their respective places.

Although when she'd first started her job, Mia had planned to eat alone after he and Bailey had finished, it seemed natural to ask her to join them and not treat her like hired help.

They settled into their chairs and began to eat. Before her, his mom had cooked for the family. Left to his own devices, he and Bailey would live on tomato soup and grilled cheese sandwiches, which he enjoyed, but it wasn't exactly staple food to raise his daughter on every meal.

"Daddy?" Bailey asked, scooting her legs beneath her so she could reach the table better.

"Yes?"

"Can Mia come with you to take me to school?" she asked, her determination when she wanted something rivaling his.

"I thought we talked about this," Mia said. "Your dad is going to drive you and I'll pick you up," she said brightly, trying to convince Bailey she had the best of both worlds with the planned arrangement.

Bailey pouted, pushing out her bottom lip. "But... but..."

"But what?" Austin placed his fork down and met his daughter's gaze. It was that quivering of her bottom lip that did him in even before she replied.

"But Lisa's mom and dad are taking her. And I don't want to be the one without a mommy."

He cursed his ex with everything he had in him but kept his expression warm for his daughter. "C'mere."

She scrambled to her feet and he pulled her into him with one arm. Mia, he noticed, discreetly rose from the table and made herself busy by the sink.

"I know it's hard for you, not having your mom around, but you know how much I love you, right?" he asked.

Bailey sniffed and nodded, those big brown, damp eyes his undoing. "You and me 'gainst the world."

"Exactly." He squeezed her tighter. "But if you want Mia to come with us tomorrow, it's okay with me."

"Yay!" She threw her arms around his neck and a lump rose to his throat. He'd do anything for her. Anything.

"Thank you, Daddy! See? You can come with us!" She pushed off him and ran to Mia, barreling into her and wrapping her little arms around Mia's waist.

Mia met his gaze, green eyes the color of a grassy field locking onto him, a smile on her beautiful face.

"Will you come?" Bailey asked.

"I wouldn't miss it," she promised his daughter.

He closed his eyes and recommitted himself to viewing her as a caregiver and not a sexy woman with just enough curves to make his mouth water and green eyes he could drown in.

★　★　★

MIA WALKED INTO the elementary school with a cobblestone façade alongside Austin and Bailey. The little girl hopped her way inside, excited to meet her teacher and be with her friends. Though it broke Mia's heart the way she was afraid she'd be the only girl without a mom there, once Austin had agreed to Mia going along, she'd seemed to put all sad thoughts out of her head.

Mia wished she'd had a father who cared as much about her as Bailey's did. Though she had been in good foster homes, it wasn't the same thing as a parent who loved you.

She centered herself, her attention back on Bailey, where it belonged. As she entered the room, she was immediately struck by the brightly decorated walls. Letters and pictures were scattered around, welcoming to all the children.

After they'd settled Bailey into her desk and warned her not to glare at Josh, who was, in fact, sitting in front of her, Austin knelt down, made certain his daughter was comfortable and happy before kissing her good-bye.

She glanced at Bailey. "So I'll be outside when school is over to pick you up," Mia reminded her, not for the first time. She didn't want the little girl to worry about who would be waiting for her when the day ended.

"I know." Bailey looked around the room, already eager for her class to get started.

Austin tipped his head toward the door, indicating it was time for them to leave.

Mia followed him into the hall. She didn't miss the way some of the other mothers glanced at Austin appreciatively, eyeing both his handsome face and, yes, his spectacular ass. Which Mia, as his employee, should not be ogling. Or noticing. Or allowing herself to think about. But she did. Often.

The question she often asked herself was, did he think about her the same way? He was respectful, always, but she sometimes caught him studying her in that inscrutable way he had. As a bodyguard, he was probably trained not to let his emotions show and he didn't. Yet she couldn't help but wonder if the attraction was mutual.

"Mia?" he asked.

"Yes?" She jerked her gaze away and looked to the floor, hoping he hadn't caught her staring or thinking inappropriate thoughts.

"Can I talk to you outside?" he asked.

She nodded. "Sure." She followed him through the double doors and they paused on the walkway on the side of the building where they'd exited. They walked toward their vehicles, which were parked side by side so he could go straight to work.

He paused by the SUV she used to drive Bailey around and do errands. "Is everything okay?" she asked.

He met her gaze, his chocolate gaze warm on hers. At that intense look, her nipples stood at attention, making her grateful for the sweater she wore that covered the evidence.

"I just wanted to thank you," he began. "Not for doing your job, which I'm extremely pleased with, by the way, but for being there for Bailey on a whole different level."

The compliment on her work made her happy. Mia loved children and she really didn't have to try very hard in order to work at her job. Bailey, especially, made it easy. "She's a special little girl."

"Yes, well, I think so, obviously," he said with a chuckle. "But most people would do the bare minimum required of them and I can tell you care about her. That's worth everything to me. To know the person who's with my child all day really puts thought and care into her feelings, not just her basic welfare and needs."

He rubbed the back of his neck as he spoke, clearly uncomfortable with their serious conversation, but she appreciated him expressing the sentiments.

"Thank you. She's a joy."

Their gazes met again, locking for a moment in what felt like a heated caress, not just a casual glance. His gaze drifted to her lips before he cleared his throat and looked away.

This was one of those times where she wondered if he was thinking about her, because she was definitely lost in thought about him. Specifically about kissing those full lips, wondering if his kiss would be hard and demanding or whisper soft. Either would work for her.

"I need to get to work," he said gruffly, breaking into her naughty thoughts.

Her cheeks burned as she dug for her keys in her purse.

"See you when you get home," she murmured without looking his way.

She headed to the driver's-side door, away from Austin, just as a group of women walked by, their voices carrying. "She's not the only nanny here but she's the youngest," one of the women said in an indiscreet loud voice.

"And he's pretty hot himself," another said. "And single."

"Think they're having an affair?"

Mia cringed at their insinuation, especially given where her mind had been seconds before. Still, women could be nasty and this group was pretty gossipy and rude. Couldn't she just have a job without being accused of screwing her boss?

Ignoring them, she climbed into the seat and slammed the door shut, closing herself inside before she could hear the conclusion the women drew. Especially since it probably matched her deepest, darkest hidden desire for Austin Rhodes.

★　★　★

AUSTIN WAITED FOR Mia to pull the SUV out of the parking spot in the school parking lot and head home before doing the same, turning his car toward the highway. He drove to the Alpha Security office, his mind on his daughter's first full day of elementary school. Kindergarten had been half day, and he hoped she was up to a complete seven hours in first grade, but he reassured himself that Bailey was his Energizer Bunny. She would rise to the challenge and even dance her way through it. He grinned at the thought. She always made him smile.

Yesterday's assignment and his daughter's need to have him around cemented the fact that he wanted to change up what he did for Alpha Security, and he had an appointment to talk to Dan this morning.

Before he could continue along that train of thought, his cell rang and his mother's name popped up on the dashboard screen.

He answered the call on speaker as he drove. "Hey, Mom."

"How did my baby do going into school today?" Sarah asked.

"Went in like a champ." He smiled, proud of his kid. "Of course, it helped that Mia joined us," he said, giving credit where it was due. "Unfortunately, Bailey had a little breakdown over the fact that her friends had their mothers bringing them into school, too."

His mom sighed. "We knew you'd have to deal with that one day."

"I did. But it was amazing how agreeing to let Mia join us changed her whole mood. She really likes her and Mia is amazing with Bailey. She's patient and loving. It's not just a job for her," he said, basically repeating what he'd said to Mia a few minutes earlier.

Mia, who'd stared at him with wide eyes and flushed cheeks, and put dirty thoughts in his head just by looking at him for a few seconds too long. He'd used those seconds to stare at her luscious mouth and wonder whether she tasted sweet like the sugar she put in her tea at night and coffee in the morning. Yes, he fucking studied her personal habits and memorized what she liked.

"Not to mention she's young and pretty?" his mother asked as if reading his mind about Mia.

"Mom!" he said, horrified she'd even go there. He felt guilty enough for his inappropriate thoughts. Now he had to worry about whether he'd sent out inadvertent signals about his interest in Mia that his mother had picked up on.

"What? I'm just pointing out that you're a healthy man with… appetites and she's a sweet, good-looking woman," his mother said, not backing down.

Jesus. He pulled behind a car driving below the

speed limit, glanced in the mirror, and swerved into the left lane to drive around it.

"She's my daughter's nanny," he reminded his mother as well as himself, because he clearly needed a good talking to. "And I just said Mia was fantastic. I'm not going to mess up a good situation for Bailey."

Not to mention, he knew better than to get involved with a woman right now. He'd been screwed by his ex and he had no desire to deal with the opposite sex on any level but professional.

Liar.

"Shut the fuck up," he muttered aloud to his inner voice.

"What did you say?" his mother asked. "I couldn't hear you."

He shook his head, grateful she'd missed those words, and swallowed hard. "I said this wasn't a conversation I want to have."

"I think you protest too much." His mother clicked her tongue like she would when he was a child. "It's not healthy to be without companionship. I don't want to know what you're doing about your sex life but—"

"Mom!" This time he yelled, feeling his face flush and having a hard time keeping an eye on the road. "This conversation is over." It reminded him of the time she'd given him the sex talk while driving on a highway and he couldn't escape. "I love you but we're done. I'll talk to you later."

"We're coming to visit this weekend," she said, reminding him of plans they'd made.

"Right. Okay. Bye for now." He disconnected quickly, shaking his head.

God love his mother. She meant well but she liked to meddle in the name of worrying about her children.

But she'd put the thought of Mia squarely at the forefront of his mind. He'd definitely lied when he told himself he had no desire for any woman. He had a healthy sex drive and he'd already admitted he wanted Mia. And the more he watched her interact with his child, the more she engaged him on many levels.

But he wouldn't be the guy who screwed the nanny. And being single didn't make it all right. She worked for him, so any kind of overture would be considered sexual harassment, and that was a lawsuit waiting to happen. And as he'd already said, he refused screw up something that worked well for his daughter. As always, she came first.

Before his dick, that was for certain. Which meant he was going to have to put a leash on his wayward thoughts, his probably not-so-subtle glances and desire to kiss her, touch her soft skin, and fuck her notwithstanding. With great difficulty, he turned his thoughts to work and his upcoming conversation with his boss, prepping himself for the pitch he was about to give.

He walked into the offices of Alpha Security. Everyone was out on assignment, so he headed directly up to Dan's office, bypassing the empty game room Dan had built for his employees to relax in during their downtime.

He knocked on Dan's door just as he was putting the phone down. "Come on in," his boss said, gesturing for Austin to join him.

"Hey. Thanks for working around me today."

Dan nodded. "Of course. When you asked to meet, it sounded important." He motioned to the chair in front of his desk.

Austin settled in while Dan leaned against the wall close by. "Talk to me, son." He considered all his employees his kids, even if only one of them was actually his biological child.

Austin drew a fortifying breath. "I know you've been talking about delegating your responsibilities because you want to cut back some. And I don't want to be out in the line of fire when I have a young child at home and I'm the only parent she has."

Dan studied him in silence, nodding as Austin spoke.

He sweated a little, worried his boss would think he was presumptuous. "I was hoping to take over some of your workload… It would take me out of the field and I could do much of the administrative side from home. I have a high-tech office setup there that would connect to the office."

"Yes."

"I'm well versed in all our clients and how the office runs, and—"

"No need for the hard sell. I said yes," Dan said with a grin. "I have two new guys coming on board to replace Ben for short-term work now that he's off guarding Summer on tour," he said of the man who'd just re-fallen for a woman who was destined to be a major pop star. "And Shane really is based out of Texas. He just does freelance here, so it was time. We'll have coverage for you on a day-to-day basis."

Austin rose from his chair. "I don't know what to say."

"You're going to help me cut back. It's me who has to say thank you." Dan held out his hand and Austin accepted it.

"I won't let you down."

Dan smiled in that fatherly way he had. "Your daughter comes first, Austin. I, of all people, understand that." Dan had raised his son, Jared, and when Ava Talbott, one of their team, was a teenager and her own mother had issues, he'd taken her in and raised her like his own. Dan understood the importance of family.

"You and I can start going through how things around here run. We'll get you spending more time at home as soon as possible."

It wasn't until the ride home, when he had more time to think, than he realized the one drawback to his brilliant plan. Time at home with Bailey meant time at home with Mia. Alone time, since his kid was in school full time. And wouldn't that wreak havoc on his plan not to think about her sexually or otherwise unless it related to his daughter.

★ ★ ★

A WEEK AFTER Bailey started school, ballet classes began. Mia ran errands for the better part of the afternoon, doing food shopping and getting Austin's dry cleaning before picking up Bailey from the small studio. The little girl looked adorable in her pink leotard, tights, and ballet slippers, her silky hair pulled back into a ponytail.

They drove home, Bailey in a booster in the back seat.

"How was class?" Mia asked.

"Good! I learned first position." She kicked the back of the front car seat, trying to get her little feet into the pose.

"You can show me when we get home. I bet your

dad will want to see, too." Mia glanced in the rearview mirror before refocusing on the road.

She pulled onto the street and caught sight of a black sedan parked at the end of the road. She'd seen the car earlier in the week and again this morning and had thought it was odd. This street was far off the highway and didn't get a lot of stray cars.

"What's for dinner?" Bailey asked. "'Cause I'm hungry. Can I have a snack when we get home?" She rattled off questions and statements like they were demands.

"What happened to please?" Mia asked. "You can have a healthy snack before dinner, like baby carrots. And your dad mentioned wanting to bring in pizza, so that's what we're having."

"Can I have hummus with the carrots? Please?"

As Mia pulled into the driveway, she turned to see Bailey with her hands clasped together in supplication. For hummus. "A little bit."

Mia unhooked the booster seat and Bailey scrambled out of the car, then Mia grabbed some grocery bags for her first trip into the house. No sooner had she entered than she realized the air conditioning seemed to have stopped working what must have been hours earlier, because the inside of the house was too hot.

She put the bags on the counter and finished emptying the SUV of groceries before calling Austin on his cell phone. He was on his way home and said he'd get the repairman on the phone as soon as he hung up with her.

Mia glanced at Bailey, who was dancing around the kitchen in long sleeves and tights. "Let's change into cooler clothes, okay?"

"Can I wear my bathing suit?" Bailey asked, her brown eyes sparkling with delight.

Mia laughed. "Why not? Just don't expect to go swimming."

"We can pretend to swim. Can I change my Barbies into bathing suits, too?"

"I don't know. Do you have homework to do first?" she asked.

Bailey scrunched her nose in reply. "A little."

"Okay, homework first, then you can play with your dolls."

"But it's ho-o-t," she whined, finally bringing up the obvious as a complaint, probably because Mia had just asked her to do something she didn't want to do.

"And you'll be in your bathing suit so you won't be as uncomfortable." She ruffled the top of the child's head. "Let's go change."

"Will you put on a bathing suit, too?" Bailey asked.

"No," Mia said. "That wouldn't be appropriate."

"What's 'propriate mean?" Bailey asked as they

headed for the stairs leading to Austin's and Bailey's rooms on the second level.

Mia had a bedroom off the kitchen on the first floor, a relief since she didn't have to worry about running into Austin when she was coming in or out of the bathroom in the upstairs hall after a shower. She had her own private one right outside her room downstairs. Being in a room near his would only make the building desire she felt for the man so much worse.

Mia bit the inside of her cheek to distract herself from her thoughts. "Appropriate means it's not the right thing to do," she explained to Bailey.

Not when Austin would be arriving home any minute. She saved her bikinis for her private time. She couldn't possibly play dress-up—or dress down as the case might be with Bailey. Mia couldn't handle Austin's eyes on her when she was half dressed. No doubt her body would betray her and his knowing gaze would zero in on her hard nipples caused by a hot glance.

She pulled her hair off the back of her sweaty neck. No matter how uncomfortably hot she was, her thoughts making things worse, she wouldn't be flaunting her body in front of her sexy boss.

Chapter Two

GOING HOME TO no air conditioning wasn't the way Austin had planned to celebrate his good news. The AC people would be over later to fix the unit, so he'd have to deal in the meantime. He pulled into the garage, turned off the engine, and walked into the house, the sound of the alarm beep drowned out by music playing.

He stepped inside, feeling the heat immediately. Damn, it was a hot September. He glanced down the hall into the kitchen, where his daughter was wearing a bathing suit and standing in a ballet pose, arms above her head.

"Like this. See? Copy me," she said to Mia, who complied, her legs contorting into whatever position Bailey demanded.

Legs he couldn't stop staring at. Strong calves, tanned from playing outside with his daughter and long enough to wrap around his waist while he pounded into her. Way not to think about her that way, he thought, annoyed with himself.

He adjusted his dick and waited in silence until they were finished dancing, giving his body a chance to calm down before announcing himself.

After Bailey twirled around and curtsied, Austin stepped out of the shadows, clapping. "Great job!"

"Daddy!"

She ran to him, and as usual, he scooped her into his arms. "Tell me about your first day of dance class. Looks like you already learned something."

He listened to her chattering, paying attention so he'd know when to nod, understanding he wouldn't be getting a word in edgewise and his mind still preoccupied with Mia.

"Who's ready for me to order pizza?" she asked as she shut the music off on her phone.

"Can I have plain?" Bailey asked. "I don't like the roni things Daddy likes."

"Pepperoni," he said, "and it's delicious." He tapped her nose. "Order half plain," he said to Mia. "I'll be back down in a few minutes." He placed Bailey down and he started for the stairs.

"Austin?" Mia called out.

"Yes?"

"Did you see a car parked on the end of the street when you came home? It was there all day and I just thought it was odd."

He shook his head. "I came in the back way. I'll go out to the front door and take a look," he said, his stomach suddenly in knots for reasons he couldn't put into words.

When he stepped onto the porch and looked down the street, a black car was sitting on the corner, too far away for him to grab the license plate. Not that he had a reason to run down the plate. But any time something odd went on, his thoughts and fears always turned to his ex-wife.

She made it a habit to hit him up for money, both when they were married and when she'd left him the first time. It wouldn't be odd for her to want something and scope out the lay of the land before approaching him.

He narrowed his gaze on the car in the distance. The sedan wasn't in front of his house but alongside a copse of trees on a common area where people weren't allowed to be build homes. The car suddenly pulled away from the curb, did a half turn, and drove off the street.

He shut the door behind him but the uneasy feeling remained. Pushing it aside for now, he headed upstairs to change into a pair of sweats and a tee shirt and wash up before dinner.

A little while later, they were seated around the

dinner table. Everyone's stomachs were full from pizza and their ears from Bailey's chatter.

"I have news," Austin said, his gaze on his daughter. "I changed my schedule up at work, and in a few weeks, I'll be working from home. No more weird late-night hours." He glanced at Mia, who toyed with her food, finding he couldn't read her expression or thoughts on the matter.

"Yay!" Bailey clapped her hands. "You can play with me when you're home!"

He met Mia's now amused gaze. "Ummm, I'll be working and you'll be in school, but if you need me, I'll be here. And no more missed dinners." Or danger, which was the key reason for the change, not that he'd mention that to his six-year-old.

"That sounds good," Mia said, but she bit down on her bottom lip, clearly taken aback by the news.

"Don't worry. I won't be under foot. My boss will keep me plenty busy and I'll be going into the office for regular meetings."

Her lips twitched in a half smile. "If you say so," she said somewhat neutrally, although he heard the uncertainty in her tone.

If he were a betting man, he'd say she'd come to the same conclusion he already had. With Bailey in school, they'd be around each other more. Alone without a buffer, making it that much more difficult to keep any simmering feelings under wraps.

★   ★   ★

THE WEEK FLEW by and the weekend arrived. From high eighties, the temperature had fallen to the midsixties, typical Connecticut fall weather. Unusually, Mia had Friday night, Saturday, and Sunday to herself. Although she was on call if Austin needed her. Today, Bailey's grandparents were here to visit, and Austin and his parents took Bailey and her friend Lisa for an early morning at the Bronx Zoo before the lines became crazy.

Mrs. Rhodes had extended an invitation but Mia didn't feel right intruding on family time if they didn't need her to work, and they insisted they didn't. The last thing she wanted to do was join them and pretend to be like the big, happy family they weren't. She knew her place and she planned to stay there no matter how hard it was slowly becoming.

She slept in and then decided to take a walk around the neighborhood in the gorgeous fresh air, something that had become a ritual while Bailey was in school. As she rounded the corner where that odd black car had parked earlier in the week, she was relieved to see it was no longer there.

She would love to walk a dog on her trips around the block, but it wasn't her place to suggest a pet to

Austin. Even if she did think a puppy would be good for Bailey. One of the foster homes she'd lived in had a mixed-breed dog that had slept at the foot of her bed. She knew many people weren't as lucky as she was in foster care, which was the reason she wanted a big family of kids someday. Kids she rescued from the system as she hadn't been.

She rounded the corner back to the house, unnerved to now see the same car idling on the corner, only to have it pull away as she reappeared on the street. She rushed inside and shut the door behind her, heart racing but she didn't know why. She'd just have to mention the car to Austin again.

She headed to shower and she changed into a comfortable pair of black leggings and an oversized shirt. She skipped makeup and pulled her hair into a messy wet bun on top of her head.

Austin texted her to let her know they were on their way home, and she walked downstairs to put out the cold cuts, bread, and salads for lunch.

Soon after, the alarm chime went off, announcing their return. The side door opened and the girls tumbled in, giggling and laughing, the adults behind them.

"Mia! We saw gorillas!" Bailey yelled, her excitement making her voice carry.

"They were so funny," Lisa said, a grin on her face.

Mr. and Mrs. Rhodes walked in behind the girls, followed by Austin. A baseball cap was backwards on his head and he wore a casual sweatshirt and jeans, a delicious look for the man usually in black slacks and white dress shirt she considered his work uniform. She tore her gaze from his sexy self and glanced at his parents. They were a good-looking couple, making it easy to see where Austin got his looks, and they were warm and sweet, and it was obvious how much they doted on their granddaughter.

"Tell me about gorillas!" Mia said, catching Austin's shake of the head and finger over his lips too late.

Oops, guess she wasn't supposed to ask that.

"The gorilla was playing with his privates!" Bailey said on a shriek, followed by uncontrollable laughter—hers, Lisa's, and even Austin's parents'.

To her shock, a red flush tinted Austin's cheeks. His daughter had embarrassed him. Oh my God, how adorably sexy.

She swallowed hard. "Okay, come settle down and eat and you can tell me about the other animals you saw," she said to the girls. Hopefully the others were better-behaved than the gorillas.

Austin shot her a thankful glance, laughter dancing in his eyes. She grinned and that sexual attraction simmered along her nerve endings.

"Mia, you really should have come along. It was

fun to see the various animals. You would have enjoyed it," Sarah Rhodes said, her voice kind.

She had short, dark hair and brown eyes that reminded Mia of her son's, while Austin was the spitting image of his father, John, but the older man's eyes were a mossy green. If his father was anything to go by, Austin would age well, not that she'd had any doubt.

"I appreciate it but I had a nice morning. It was good for Bailey to be with her family." She smiled at the other woman.

"Mia, this looks wonderful. Thank you," Austin's dad said, walking over to the counter where she'd set out a variety of options for lunch. "Let's eat!"

Mia laughed as the girls beat him to the counter, grabbing plates and putting together their sandwiches.

"You snooze, you lose, Dad." Austin glanced at the girls. "Easy on the mustard, Bailey Button," he warned just as she squirted too much onto her bread.

"I'll help them," his mother said.

With all the commotion, the sound of the doorbell was muffled, but Mia picked up on it, as did Austin, his gaze flickering with a question toward the front of the house.

"I'll get it!" Mia walked out of the room and strode to the door. "Who is it?"

When no one answered, she peeked out the side

glass pane and saw a woman impatiently pacing back and forth. She opened the door partway. "Can I help you?"

An attractive brunette with a cool stare met her gaze. "I want to see my daughter."

Mia went mute. Nothing had prepared her for the eventuality of Austin's ex, Bailey's mother, showing up on their doorstep and demanding access to her daughter. Wearing a bandage-style dress that was more appropriate for a nightclub than a visit with her child, she assessed Mia, looking her up and down. Considering she'd dressed down, as she always did for her job, she doubted this woman found anything worth noting.

She swallowed hard, her hand still on the edge of the door, not opening it entirely. "I'll have to talk to Austin."

"Austin is it? And just who the hell are you?"

Mia straightened her shoulders. "I'm the nanny."

"Really," she said with a disbelieving snort.

"Mia? Who's at the door?" Before she could reply, Austin came up behind her, his big, warm body solid behind hers. "Kayla? What the fuck are you doing here?"

"Daddy, who's here? Are we having company? Can I say hi?" Bailey's little voice sounded from behind them and Austin stiffened.

"Is that my Bailey?" Kayla asked, taking a step

forward.

"Get Bailey out of here now," Austin said harshly in Mia's ear.

His body language, his tone of voice vibrated with barely leashed anger he obviously didn't want his daughter to hear or see. No more than he wanted to see his ex-wife.

Mia swung around him, scooped Bailey into her arms, and brought her back into the kitchen with her grandparents.

She mouthed who the visitor was to Austin's parents, and they helped her keep Bailey busy. Mia needed the same distraction. She only wished she could be a fly on the wall to hear what was going on between Austin and his ex-wife outside.

AUSTIN STARED AT his ex, furious that she'd show up on his doorstep without warning. Asking to see the little girl she'd mistreated was just ammunition to make him even angrier.

He pulled the door closed behind him so Bailey couldn't hear and faced Kayla on the front porch. First impressions mattered and one look at her in a skanky dress and heels told him she wasn't here to kneel down and hug the child she hadn't seen in two years.

"What are you doing here?" he asked, folding his

arms across his chest.

"I think that's obvious. I want to see my daughter." But there was nothing maternal in her voice or her demeanor. There was calculating going on behind those eyes. He was sure of it.

"Try again." He blocked the door with his body, lest she get some bright idea about trying to push past him.

She hadn't wanted to be Bailey's mother to begin with. Having a baby, then a toddler was too much work, too hard when she'd rather be partying and spending money.

She stepped closer, the cloying scent of her perfume too familiar and unwelcome. "Come on, Austin. Let me come in. We have a lot of catching up to do." She followed up her words by trailing her fingers up his chest in a faked seduction attempt neither of them were really buying.

Yep. She wanted something.

"Where's Marco?" he asked of the man she'd left him for, a bottom-feeder who was only too happy to live off the settlement Austin had given her when they divorced.

She pulled off her sunglasses and met his stare. "We broke up."

He narrowed his gaze. "Don't tell me you ran through the settlement money."

"It wasn't enough and you know it," she said, pouting like a child.

"It was plenty when you grabbed it in exchange for custody. Which I have. Sole custody," he reminded her. "So don't expect to come sniffing around Bailey now. She's happier without you." Because her mother couldn't be bothered to pay enough attention to her to keep her safe. He cringed at the reminder.

She shook her head. "Don't fool yourself. Courts take pity on mothers. Especially ones who were coerced into giving up custody in the first place by their ex-husband. The situation wasn't at all fair and I'll have no problem telling my story in court." She blinked up at him, the fake tears in her eyes a definite threat.

"What do you want?" he asked past gritted teeth. Although he already knew.

She wanted more money to go away and leave Bailey alone.

"Pay me," she said, confirming his hunch. "You owe me for screwing up my body to give birth in the first place."

He pinched the bridge of his nose. There was no way in hell he'd let her near his child. The problem with paying her was if he gave in now, there would be no end to her blackmail in the future. Every time she ran low on cash, she'd return with the same threat of taking him to court to regain her parental rights with a bullshit sob story.

She was a very good actress. Good enough to convince a judge she was a loving mother who'd had her child wrongfully taken away in the first place. Hadn't he fallen for her claims of love, of having gotten pregnant by accident, of them being in it together… until she was ready to admit to the truth? Pins in his condoms worked wonders. Kayla was a classic walking, talking cliché and he'd fallen for every one of her tricks.

He schooled his face into a bored mask, refusing to show her how much her threat rattled him. "I'm not paying you, Kayla. You got your settlement." But he needed time to think of a better plan.

She shook her head and smiled. "You will. You'll walk back inside, take one look at the little girl who looks just like you, and you'll do anything to keep her away from me. I can wait for you to come around." She patted his cheek and he flinched at her unwanted touch.

"Go away."

She treated him to a patronizing wink. "Just don't take too long. I might get bored and go talk to a lawyer and tell him your girlfriend is a little young. As well as everything else I mentioned." She pivoted on her heel and strode away.

He didn't bother correcting her that Mia was the nanny. "Bitch," he muttered under his breath. He stood outside for another solid five minutes, breathing in the cool air. He needed the time to calm the fuck down before heading inside and facing his daughter.

★ ★ ★

NOBODY TALKED ABOUT Bailey's mother's visit, at least not that Mia heard. The adults were careful of her little, always attentive ears. She was immediately distracted by dessert after her sandwich and she never even asked who was at the door earlier. But Austin had been stressed and on edge for the rest of the afternoon.

Mia took the girls outside to play on the big wooden swing set in the yard, and she was certain Austin used the time to fill his parents in on whatever had gone on with his ex. Her heart went out to him because he'd definitely been anxious and off ever since.

Luckily, Bailey fell asleep early and easily thanks to the morning walking around the zoo and the afternoon outside. Mia had a small television in her room and was going to watch TV, but she wanted a cup of tea first, so she headed to the kitchen, surprised to find Austin sitting in the dark.

"Do you mind?" she asked softly, her hand on the

light switch.

"Go ahead." She turned on the overheads.

He sat in one of the kitchen chairs, looking rumpled and sexy, his hair standing on end from his hand running through it, a pair of track pants on his hips, and no shirt covering his upper body. Her gaze locked on the sexy tattoo trailing up one arm, from his wrist up to, and over, his shoulder, his bare, muscular chest causing flutters in her belly.

"I was just going to get tea. Can I make you some?" she asked. "I picked up some chamomile. It might help you relax." She guessed the reason he sat in the kitchen was stress over today's mess with his ex.

"Why not? Nothing else is helping."

She pulled two mugs from the counter. One of the things she appreciated about this job was the easy instant hot attached to the sink. No taking time to boil water for a cup of hot tea.

"Sugar or milk?" she asked him.

"Plain. Like my coffee."

She added water, dropped the teabags in the cups, and put sugar in hers only. "I'm a good listener," she offered, placing his mug in front of him on the table. "And unloading might help your blood pressure a lot more than the tea."

She waited for him to meet her gaze and nod before joining him, settling into the chair beside his.

"I'm not really sure where to begin."

She shrugged. "Try the beginning. I find it's the simplest place."

A reluctant smile tugged at his mouth. He was so serious and intense, she braced herself and waited for him to find the words to explain.

"I wasn't in love with Kayla," he said at last. "We'd barely been dating a month, but she got pregnant. I thought since we were in it together, I should step up and do the right thing," he said.

She let her tea sit and cool off while she listened, more interested than she should be about his history, for personal reasons more than professional curiosity. She cared about him and his daughter. "Sounds admirable," she said.

He scrubbed a hand over his face, rubbing his eyes. "Maybe. But the thing is, we weren't in it together. She got pregnant on purpose and didn't tell me until after we were married and things went to hell. I guess she thought my job was exciting and I had money to keep her happy." He snorted at that. "There was nothing happy about her."

Mia winced, shocked any woman would trap a man—outside a television soap opera, that is. "Why wasn't she at least satisfied if she'd gotten what she wanted from you?" Mia asked, wondering about the ex-Mrs. Rhodes, who she disliked more with everything she learned about her.

"She bitched about the way the baby changed her body and she was miserable. She once told me she'd made a mistake poking holes in the condoms but she was too far into the pregnancy to do anything about it." He paused and met Mia's gaze. "I thank God for that fact every day."

"I know you do." She *knew* how much he adored his daughter, but inside she was disgusted by any woman who could manipulate a good man like Austin. And to then complain about her situation? She couldn't comprehend it.

"I'm sure you're curious, so here's the rest of it. We made the marriage work for two years. And she left me and Bailey for a rich guy she met at the gym… until he got bored, dumped her ass, and she came back. She said all the right things about having learned her lesson and wanting to be a real mom this time. So I took her back for Bailey's sake."

He braced a hand on the table and glanced over. "God, I was such an asshole."

"No." She pulled her chair closer to his, the warm scent of his aftershave hitting her without warning, powerful, hot, and sexy. All the wrong things to be thinking about now, while he was baring his soul.

"Want to know what I think?" she asked in a husky voice she hoped didn't betray her yearning. She didn't wait for his reply. "I think you're a great dad who would do anything for his daughter. That's something to be proud of, not to beat yourself up over."

He shook his head and let out a pained laugh. "Well, it's a mistake I won't make again. Not with anyone, but especially not with Kayla. She doesn't have the patience or the temperament to be a parent. But thank you for saying that about me." He lifted the mug and gave her a sexy half-smile.

She glanced away. Not sexy. Just a smile. Jeez. She couldn't contain her thoughts around him for one single second.

"But I do want you to know the reason she can't be allowed near Bailey again." He took a sip of the hot tea, drew his tongue over his lips, a movement she couldn't help but follow.

"Bailey was four... almost five," he said, bringing her back to focus on what was important. "As far as I know, and hope, too young to remember. I worked late and Kayla was home. Bailey's schedule was pretty much the same as now except for the fact that it's later now. And she tries to negotiate harder."

"She's good at brokering a deal."

He shook his head and laughed, but he quickly sobered, his expression turning dark. "She was... is... precocious. All I know is the morning after that night,

I helped her get dressed for the day and she had finger marks on her arm. Adult-sized red marks," he said through clenched teeth. "I asked her what happened. She said, and I can still hear the words, clear as day, 'Mommy did this,' followed by big crocodile tears." He rubbed his palm against his eyes and she ducked her head, giving him a moment of privacy.

Nausea filled her at the thought of anyone hurting that child, let alone her mother. "I'm sorry," she whispered after a moment.

"Yeah, me, too. Sorry I gave her a second chance. Sorrier I didn't document it. Kayla didn't deny it, either. Said Bailey wasn't getting dressed fast enough, was giving her a hard time, so she grabbed her—hard enough to bruise—and forced her into the pajamas."

"What did you do?" Mia was almost afraid to ask.

"Saw a lawyer, had custody, divorce, and settlement papers drawn up, handed her a check for one hundred grand, and told her to get the hell out and never come back."

Mia swallowed hard. "Yet she showed up today."

"My guess? She ran out of cash. She's threatening to sue for custody and tell the judge a sob story about how I forced her out of her daughter's life... unless I pay up. But if I do that, I'll keep paying, and that's sure as hell not how this is going to go down." His grip was so tight on the mug his knuckles turned white.

"I won't let her near Bailey."

He met her gaze, his deadly serious. "You see her, you hear from her, you call me."

She nodded. "I will. I promise," she said. "Do you think that black car on the street was her?" she asked.

He shook his head. "She had a blue rental today. Maybe she hired someone to watch the house. But that wouldn't jibe with her running low on cash." He shrugged. "I don't know but I'm going to find out," he said, his stress still obvious.

"It's going to be okay." She placed what she meant to be a comforting hand on his arm, hoping to calm him. But it was the first time she'd touched him and the sizzling shock ran straight through her body.

He glanced at her hand and she froze, meeting his gaze. The warmth of his skin seeped into her palm and the heated look in his eyes wrapped around her body like a caress. Physically there was no doubt she desired him but every warning in her brain told her to walk away before either of them did something stupid, and from the darkened hue of his brown eyes, she wasn't alone in the wanting.

But she had a good job for a man she respected and a little girl she adored. She'd be a fool to let lust get in the way of common sense and living a smart life. Quietly and with his hot gaze on hers, she slid her hand off him.

Shooting him a regret-filled look, she picked up her tea and made her way to bed.

Alone.

Chapter Three

SEPTEMBER WENT BY quickly with no word from Kayla, which made Austin nervous. His lawyer said they could take her apart on the stand if it ever got that far. As time passed, Austin became convinced that his ex-wife was more afraid she would be awarded custody than he was of going up against her in court. That was the hope he held on to as he tried to push her to the back of his mind.

Dan had held up his end of the bargain, and by late September, Austin was working three days a week from home, at the office one day for the weekly meeting, and a second when needed. An intended result of his time at the house was more ability to be on call when parents were requested in class. Bailey's school was big on "Days of the Year" celebrations, and once a week the teacher allowed parents in with the kids.

Today was a celebration of Stanley Berenstain's

birthday, the children's book author and illustrator, and Bailey had volunteered Austin as one of the parents who would read to the kids this afternoon. Unfortunately an office emergency came up and he had to go in to work, so Mia was going to read for him. Bailey had taken the news in stride, no doubt because she had Mia to take his place.

Mia, who he couldn't stop thinking about and not as his child's nanny. She captivated him with her sexy body. Her easy grace, her kindness… everything about her called to him. He wanted to taste her, to feel her curves beneath him. It was quickly becoming an obsession.

She knew him now, took care of him as well as his kid. Each morning she had his coffee—black the way he'd mentioned he liked it—ready for him before he went to work or headed upstairs to his office. But things had changed.

On the night he'd confided in her about his ex-wife, the night she'd reached out and touched him for the first time, he'd known the awareness between them was mutual. Why else would she have fled the kitchen, her cheeks on fire, unable to meet his gaze?

And ever since, it was as if a wall had fallen between them. Maybe it was his imagination but she was more relaxed around him now, less formal. The sharing of his personal pain and her comforting touch had both bonded them and crossed a line neither of them wanted to acknowledge.

They locked eyes often now. They brushed past each other with inadvertent touches he'd never noticed before but couldn't stop thinking about when he was alone.

Nighttime was painful, as he'd lie in his bed, knowing she was one floor down while he was hot and worked up, wanting her and unable to have her. Showers were worse, but at least then he could make good use of his hand, his mind conjuring images of her naked, kneeling at his feet, her lips around his cock.

It was fucking unbearable, considering there was still that defined line between employer and employee keeping them apart. And he understood, at least on a rational level, that for both their sakes, there had to be one.

He wrapped up things at the office more quickly than anticipated and he decided to surprise Bailey at school. He arrived midway through the reading hour, signed in at the office, and headed to the classroom. He walked down the hallways, cheery only due to the brightly colored drawings done by the children, and approached the room.

The door was open, and as he drew closer, Mia's voice traveled toward him. She read about Mama Bear,

Sister Bear, and Grizzly Gramps, her voice animated with each character she mentioned. He paused in the doorway and took in the sight.

Mia sat in the teacher's larger chair, Bailey beside her in a small one. Just as the kids who kneeled and sat on the floor eagerly listened to her rendition of the story, so, too, did his daughter, watching with adoring eyes. He was pretty riveted himself and not by the story but by the woman reading it. Her expressive eyes flashed with delight, her cheeks were alight with color, and despite wearing a sweater that covered her well, he could see the outline of those breasts he imagined cupping in his hands.

With a shake of his head, he drew his attention to the stick-figure drawings on the wall, anything to cool himself off. He waited until he heard Mia say the words, "The end," with a flourish before stepping inside. The kids clapped for her, so Austin joined them.

"Daddy! You made it!" Bailey grinned up at him from her place on the chair. Instead of running straight to him, she grabbed Mia's hand and looked up at her. "Thank you!" She gave her a big hug before heading over to him to do the same.

"Thank you for coming, Mia. And Mr. Rhodes, I'm glad you could stop by for Bailey," her teacher, Mrs. Johnson, said.

"I did my best. But I'm guessing she didn't even miss me. She had a much better reader." He grinned at Mia, who blushed at the compliment.

"Thanks for having me," she said to the teacher. "Bye, Bailey." She waved and Austin did the same as the kids all scrambled back to their desks.

"See you at home," he said.

He placed a hand on Mia's back, his palm burning at the innocent touch, as they stepped out of the room. "Thank you," he said to her.

"You're welcome but I was just a stand-in for her dad." She tucked a long strand of blonde hair behind her ear that had fallen out of her ponytail.

His fingers itched to touch those strands and see how soft her hair actually was.

He cleared his throat. "You're hardly just a stand-in." He shoved his hands into his front pockets, doing his best not to stare.

Today she wore a pair of tight-fitting jeans and that V-neck sweater, totally school appropriate, but his brain didn't want to cooperate with that fact. All he could see was her barely there cleavage and think about the luscious fullness hidden beneath. He spent hours in the gym trying not to think about what color her nipples were or whether she'd fill his hands or overflow them. Yeah, you could call him a breast man.

He started to sweat and decided a subject change

was in order.

"Want to get a cup of coffee? After sitting in on meetings for the better part of the morning, I'm dying for some caffeine."

She glanced at her watch. "I don't know. I need to be back in an hour for pickup, and if I go home, I could get dinner started."

Did she not want to be alone with him? He wasn't sure nor did he plan to take no for an answer. He wanted to know more about her and this seemed like the perfect opportunity.

"Or you could get coffee with me, I'll drop you back off here for your car and to get Bailey, and we could order in Chinese or sushi."

She narrowed her gaze. "Wow. Coffee and no cooking or going home to prep dinner. You drive a hard bargain," she said, laughing so her pretty green eyes lit up with delight.

His dick perked up at the sound. "Don't forget to factor in the good company when you're weighing your options."

"When you put it that way, how can I resist? Let's go to Starbucks."

A little while later, Austin sat across from Mia at the local Starbucks, not far from the school. She took a sip of the vanilla latte she'd ordered, ending up with cream on her upper lip. The desire to lick it off her and taste her mouth was strong. Only the fact that they were in a public place kept him sitting in his seat.

She slid her tongue over her lip, pulling the white froth into her mouth, and moaned. "Now this is a luxury," she said.

He was grateful for the table that hid his erection, because if they were standing, it would be loud and proud.

"Are you telling me I don't pay you enough?" he asked.

She laughed. "You pay me plenty. I'm just saving for my future."

He nodded in understanding. "I can respect that."

"Aren't you going to drink yours?" she asked.

He nodded. "Cheers," he said with a grin, lifting his cup before taking a sip.

She smiled and did the same.

"So I'm curious. How did you end up being a nanny? What was your path?" he asked.

She glanced at him over the top of her cup. "I was in foster care from the age of seven until I aged out at eighteen," she said.

He thought of his little girl, and the idea of her being left alone, to the clutches of the state and whatever person took her in, made his stomach turn. "I'm sorry," he said, suddenly envisioning her as a little thing like Bailey, only a few years older, going to live with strangers.

"Don't be. I mean, I had it better than most. Good families, decent people took me in. As I got older, I loved taking care of the younger kids and the babies in the houses I was in. I didn't make trouble, so I didn't get switched around too often." She shrugged, seemingly having made peace with her past.

"So you always liked kids."

She nodded. "I put myself through a local college. I majored in early child development and minored in psychology, and I could have gone on, gotten my master's in education, been a teacher…"

"I hear a *but* there," he said, enjoying the story and her attitude toward life.

She smiled. "*But* I'd been working as a nanny while I was in school, and it suited me." She shrugged. "Not a very exciting story."

"It is to me." He met her gaze, hoping to convey that he really did appreciate her life and admire her. "You're strong, Mia. And you made the best of the hand you were dealt."

She blushed. "Well, thank you for saying that."

"No thanks necessary. Just telling the truth. So what's your end game?"

She paused, lowering the cup from her lips. "You'll laugh. Or at the very least, you won't think it's overly ambitious."

He ignored his coffee, more interested in the fascinating woman sitting across from him. "Try me."

"Someday I'd like a family of my own. A lot of kids, not all mine. Kids who've been in foster care too long and never adopted because everyone wants babies." She rubbed her cup between her palms, not meeting his gaze. "See? Nothing all that enterprising, like becoming a teacher or succeeding in business."

He couldn't stop staring, enthralled not just by her beauty but by her heart. "I think it's inspiring, what you want to do." And the man by her side when she fulfilled her dreams would be one lucky SOB. "Not for me, because been there, done that… the family and marriage thing, but I'm sure it can work for the right couple." He shrugged, realizing he'd admitted way too much. "I hope you find what you're looking for," he said, meaning it.

She glanced down, her gaze sweeping over her watch on her wrist. "Oh! It's time to pick up Bailey." She crumpled the napkin beside her and picked up her cup as she rose to her feet.

He stood, joining her as they tossed their half-finished drinks in the trash. They headed to the car and he beat her there, opening the passenger door before she could grab the handle herself.

He turned back and she stopped short. He caught her before she bumped into him, grasping her around the waist and pulling her close. She sucked in a surprised breath but didn't back away, her face inches from his. Her mouth so damned close.

He knew better, he really did, but he was tired of denying himself what he wanted and his body was definitely on board. He waited for a sign she wasn't right there with him. If she pulled back or jerked away, he'd apologize and they'd move forward from there. Instead she swayed toward him, sealing her fate.

He grasped her waist, anchoring himself by touching her, the soft sweater doing little to hide her slender body or delicate curves. He tipped his head, sliding his tongue across her lips, and with a soft moan, she parted her mouth and let him inside. She tasted of vanilla and coffee, a sweet flavor that was all Mia.

Their tongues touched, tangled, and his body came alive with a hunger he hadn't known before.

She raised her arms, hands coming to his biceps, holding on for a brief second before she gave in and wrapped her arms around him, pulling him close, giving him all the excuse he needed to deepen the kiss. He tilted his head and consumed her, swirling his tongue around the farther recesses of her mouth.

He had no wall, no car door to push her against, which was a good thing because he wouldn't have been able to control himself if he crushed his body against hers. The kiss would have to do, and it went on, him lost in the scent of her, the way her breasts crushed against his chest, and the feel of her silken tongue rubbing against his own. He bit down gently on her lower lip and she moaned into his mouth, the sound going straight to his dick.

"Get a room!" someone called out, breaking the spell that had come over him and caused him to kiss her in a parking lot like they were alone in his garage.

She lifted her head and he touched his forehead to hers, needing time to catch his breath. It would be awhile before his body calmed down, his dick hard and erect in his pants.

"I should apologize," he said, not letting go of her waist. "I don't want to but I should. Because I'm your boss and I don't want you to feel taken advantage of. Or sue me for sexual harassment, God forbid." He laughed but the thought wasn't the least bit funny.

"It was mutual," she whispered. "I just don't know what to make of it. I've never crossed that line with an employer before." Her voice trembled and he hated that he'd put that quiver there.

"Listen," he began.

"No. That kiss shouldn't have happened and there won't be a repeat. It's fine." She ducked past him and slid into the car. "Let's just forget about it," she said, reaching for the handle so she could pull the door shut and seal herself inside.

He stepped back, giving her space, but his body and mind still buzzed from that simple kiss. There was something brewing between them that she couldn't discount by pretending it had never happened. Something that would bring them together again.

It wasn't like he didn't still have concerns about sleeping with his kid's nanny. He did. He just knew the desire between them was stronger than their common sense, and sooner or later, she'd come to the same conclusion.

Still, for now he'd respect her wishes and back off. But he wasn't foolish enough to think they could avoid the inevitable.

Not anymore.

MIA WAS SHAKEN by what had happened with Austin in the parking lot. She hadn't seen that kiss coming, no matter how much she might have desired it, and now that they'd crossed that line, she didn't know what to say or do except to pretend it had never happened. The hottest, most sensual kiss of her life and she had to put it behind her.

She couldn't let her mind drift into memories of how his mouth had captured hers, gently at first, his tongue gliding over her lips, his tongue tangling with hers, and then it'd turned molten, his teeth nipping at her lip, the sensation traveling straight to her core. No, she wasn't supposed to think about that at all.

Somehow she'd managed that feat for the rest of the week and tomorrow was Friday. She blew out a breath and pulled a lasagna from the oven, placing it on a cooling rack on the counter.

"Mia!" Bailey shouted, running into the kitchen from upstairs and skidding to a stop in front of her. "I was FaceTiming with Grandma and guess what? I'm going there for a sleepover tomorrow night!"

Mia smiled at the enthusiasm in her tone. "That sounds like fun."

"Will you miss me?" Bailey asked, seating herself on a stool by the counter.

Mia glanced at the little girl. "You bet I will but I'm going out with some friends tomorrow night, so that'll help me get through it." She was taking the train to New York City to see friends from her days living there for school and work.

"Like a playdate?" Bailey asked.

"Exactly."

"Hi, ladies." Austin walked into the room, his gaze zeroing in on the cooling dinner. "That smells incredible."

"Thank you." He seemed to like her cooking and it made her ridiculously happy to know she was doing something helpful for him, even if it was her job.

"Daddy, Mia has a playdate Friday night when I'm at Grandma and Grandpa's. Isn't that good? So she won't have time to miss me too much."

Although she was technically off Friday night, if she didn't go out, Bailey sometimes made her way down to her room and encouraged her to watch television with her until bedtime.

"What'll you do when I'm gone?" the precocious little girl asked.

"I'm sure I'll find something to keep me busy," Austin said wryly.

Mia didn't want to think about what Austin might do to *keep busy* on a Friday night without his daughter. No doubt the man had women he saw, discreetly, because in the time she'd been working for him, he'd never brought a female around Bailey nor had he mentioned going out. He hadn't dressed up in the evenings for a date, either. Still, that didn't mean he was celibate. Hell, his kissing skills were off the charts and that kind of thing took practice. Didn't it?

She glanced over, noting he wore his typical hanging-around-the-house outfit, black track pants and a tee shirt, and she had trouble tearing her gaze away from those muscular arms and, in particular, the one sleeve of tattoos. God, the man was sexy. And although she knew it was her imagination, she thought he'd gotten more so since their kiss and her vow to forget it had happened. It was as if the heavens were punishing her by making him look even hotter and more edible.

"So what kind of playdate do you have, Mia?" Austin asked, a handsome grin on his face as he settled into his chair at the table.

She frowned at his inquiry, not wanting to get into her personal life when she was trying to keep a professional distance from him.

Still, this was an easy question in front of Bailey. "I'm having dinner with friends."

"Female friends?" he asked, surprising her.

"Friends from my city days," she said vaguely, if only because it really was none of his business. If they were going to keep things normal, he shouldn't be asking.

She swung around, picked up oven mitts, and carried the casserole tin to the already set table.

"How are you getting there?" he asked.

She told herself this was normal conversation, not to read anything into it. Even if they'd never discussed her social life before and she had gone out on the admittedly rare Friday or Saturday night.

"The train," she said, joining them and sitting down, pulling her chair in so she was more comfortable.

He frowned at that.

"Something wrong?"

"Nothing going in. It's just a little empty and dangerous coming back alone at night."

"I'll be okay," she said, understanding his point. "I'm not coming home all that late and I'll keep my eyes open."

A growl-like noise sounded from deep in his throat. She couldn't tell if he was agreeing or still unhappy with her choice in transportation, but he didn't get a say.

"Going anywhere fun?" he asked.

"I'm meeting the girls at happy hour after my friends get off work." She caught her slip immediately. Yes, she was going with her girlfriends.

His frown turned into an obviously satisfied smile, telling her he'd have cared if she had plans with guys, too. The notion pleased her, which was ridiculous. She shouldn't care what Austin thought of her social life. They weren't going to go *there*. No repeat of the kiss. Not again.

Mia served Bailey a smaller portion of lasagna and busied herself giving Austin his before taking her own. Bailey, meanwhile, had watched the grown-ups talk in unusual silence, and now she dug into her meal quickly and with gusto, spreading the dinner all over her face.

Mia nudged her lightly. "Napkin," she said, pointing to her sauce-covered cheeks.

The child wiped her face, succeeding in smearing the red sauce around even more. With a chuckle, Mia dipped her napkin into a glass of water and wiped Bailey's mouth and cheeks.

Austin's gaze followed the interchange, his dark eyes warming at the sight.

Flustered, Mia focused on her meal. Luckily, Bailey finished her food quickly and the chatting began again, giving Mia a much-needed break from Austin's questions and concerns and her desire for a man she couldn't, shouldn't have.

★ ★ ★

IT HAD BEEN a long time since Mia had been in a bar during happy hour. The loud din of voices and laughter rang around her, and she couldn't hear her friends talk over the noise. She turned down offers from guys who wanted buy her a drink, not in the mood for small talk with strangers. She'd rather be catching up with her girls than fending off potential advances. Besides, her mind was occupied with thoughts of one man only and she couldn't get him out of her head.

From the bar, they went to a nightclub, and though there still wasn't quiet time to talk, she danced with her friends and had a great time. The night went fast, and before she realized it, it was past eleven. She wanted to grab a train home, not wait until the last one that would be completely empty.

"Hey," Amber, her good friend from her days being a nanny in Manhattan, said, having to yell in her ear. "You have that I'm-done-here look."

Mia smiled. "You know me."

"Let's go. I'll share your cab to Grand Central. I have to pass there on the way to my place anyway."

"Great!" They said good-bye to the others and she and Amber headed for the exit.

They walked through the doors and into the fresh, cool night air, the silence surrounding them a welcome relief.

"Oh my God. Peace and quiet!" Amber exclaimed.

"Tell me about it. Oh, look, there's a coffee place on the corner. Let's get something before we grab a cab."

They headed into the shop and placed their orders, sitting down to wait for them to be made. "So what's up with you? You seem a little off tonight. Not that we could talk over the noise but that's why we're here. Problems with the new job?"

Mia shook her head. "Just the opposite. It's a dream job. Great kid, nice room, access to the car, pay is good."

"Then what's wrong?"

Amber knew her well. She'd held Mia's hand and seen her through the trial with her last employer, and the wife's ranting and raving that Mia had ruined her family, even though it was her husband who'd done an illegal deed. Parker Alexander, thinking he was home alone, had a business meeting with an associate during which they discussed the kind of retirement scam that would make Bernie Madoff flinch.

Mia had heard enough to grow concerned, especially given the memory of the swindle that had cost one of her foster parents everything. Instinct had made her turn on her phone to record the conversation. And when whispers about embezzlement in Alexander Investments started to come out, she'd taken the recording to the police.

Unfortunately, due to New York law, the tape couldn't stand on its own. It had merely proven to the DA that Mia's story was true… which was why they'd subpoenaed her to testify. She'd literally had to sit in the hot seat, knowing every word she said was helping to put her former boss in prison.

"Mia? Are you going to tell me what's going on?" Amber asked.

Mia blew out a long breath. "The guy I work for? He's drop-dead gorgeous and… he kissed me." And she'd kissed him back, and she hadn't stopped daydreaming about it since.

"Whoa," Amber said, shock in her gaze. "Is this a good thing? Or a bad thing?"

"That's what I'm trying to decide."

"Mia!" the barrista called out, letting them know their coffee was ready.

"Be right back." Mia rose and picked up their cups, sitting back down in her seat across from her friend. "Here you go." She slid Amber's cup across the table and took a sip of her latte. "Ooh, it's hot."

"Okay, let's figure this out. Did you like the kiss?" she asked bluntly, as was her way.

Mia's cheeks flushed. "Umm, yes. It was the hottest kiss of my life."

"So it's the employer issue?" Amber asked knowingly.

Mia wrapped her hand around the cup. "In part." And that's what she'd been struggling so hard with. If she got past the fact that she worked for him, there were deeper issues she didn't want to think about.

Amber took a sip of her mocha-flavored coffee. "This is me you're talking to. What's going on?"

Mia swallowed hard. "He's the whole package. A sexy man, a good-hearted guy who adores his child... and his daughter is great, too."

Amber leaned closer. "This is all good! It's not like you're telling me he's a player who hits on every woman he meets. So—"

"So I can't afford to fall for him! He admitted he's done the family thing for the last time. He was burned.

Badly. But from my perspective, he has, he is everything I've ever wanted in my life." She rubbed her hands on her jeans, hating having to admit these things out loud. "So how foolish would I be to sleep with the man I work for? And possibly fall hard, knowing ahead of time that we want drastically opposite things out of life? Then I'd have to get over him while working in his home. I know that's not wise," she said, voicing her greatest fears.

Amber twirled her brown hair around one finger as she listened thoughtfully. "What if you didn't have to get over him? What if you fell for him and he fell just as hard for you?" her optimistic friend asked.

No, that wasn't in the cards. "Life hasn't typically given me the family I wanted," Mia murmured. "And he's already made it clear he isn't doing the commitment thing again."

"Then go into it for the sex. If that kiss is anything to go by, you're in for some spectacular orgasms."

"Be quiet." Mia crumpled her napkin into a ball and threw it at her friend, her face on fire from the direction of their conversation.

"Just giving you your options," Amber said unrepentantly.

"Let's just say you've given me a lot to think about and leave it at that."

Amber shrugged. "Go for the orgasms. That's all

I'm saying."

Mia rolled her eyes. "You just had to have the last word, didn't you?"

Amber grinned over her coffee cup and laughed.

They spent a few more minutes talking about Amber's life and live-in boyfriend, her job as a guidance counselor for junior high school kids, and life in general before heading to hail a cab so Mia could take the train back to Austin's house.

AUSTIN PACED HIS family room at midnight on Friday night. He'd long since dropped Bailey off at his parents' place farther upstate and, at his mother's coaxing, stayed for dinner. It wasn't like he'd had other plans, and he hadn't wanted to be home in the quiet house by himself. You'd think he'd enjoy the break from his usual routine with Bailey, and he did, but he knew if he was alone, his thoughts would turn to Mia. As they did now.

What was she doing at bars in Manhattan? How many guys tried to pick her up? Was she safe wandering Grand Central Station at night, and alone on the train ride home? He didn't need to tell himself he was obsessed. He was.

Maybe he should have gone out with the guys and Ava, his friends from work, but then he'd have had to ask his parents to drive here to get Bailey, and he didn't want to put them out. Which left him home, nursing a cold beer and wondering what Mia meant when she said she wouldn't be out late. Because in his book, after midnight was late.

He shouldn't have acted so overprotective when she'd told him she was taking the train, or worse, like an overbearing boyfriend, which he definitely was not. But thanks to his job, he was someone who considered all angles of any situation, and he always looked out for the people he cared for. And there was no doubt he cared about Mia. He glanced at the clock once more.

Finally, the alarm beep sounded at the side door, letting him know that Mia had returned. He closed his fingers around the armrests on his chair and remained in his seat. She had to pass through this room—and him—to get to her bedroom.

Having picked Bailey up from school and driven her to his folks', he hadn't been home when she left the house. So he was unprepared when she strode into the room, looking like a sexy siren wearing a pair of high wedge shoes and skintight jeans. A cropped black leather jacket completed the outfit with a sparkly low-cut shirt beneath. Her hair, normally pulled up in a messy bun, hung straight down her back, the long strands perfect for him to wrap around his hands and hold on to while he fucked her from behind.

He muffled a low groan, warning his dick not to stand at attention and give his reaction to her outfit away.

"Austin!" She raised a hand to her chest in surprise, obviously startled by his presence. She came to a stop in front of his chair. "I thought maybe you'd be out but the alarm was off so... I knew you were here. But I didn't think you'd be downstairs."

That she thought he'd have gone out tonight was interesting. He stored the fact away for later. "I'm just having a drink before I turn in."

He rose from his seat and picked up the now empty bottle, walking across the room and tossing it in the recycling bin in the kitchen before returning to talk to her.

"How'd you get back from the train?" he asked, yet another thing that had concerned him. He'd have picked her up if she'd asked, but she hadn't.

"I called an Uber. And I'm back home, safe and sound," she said, clearly meaning to reassure him.

"Did you have a nice time?" He sat on the arm of the couch.

"I did. I don't see my friends often, so it was fun." Her eyes glittered as she answered.

Obviously she'd had a good time while he sat home and brooded. About her. Had she thought about him at all? Would it have bothered her if he'd been on a date?

"Why would you think I went out?" he asked, his mind returning to her earlier statement.

"I don't know." But her cheeks flushed pink, as if she knew something and didn't want to admit to it.

"Come on, Mia. You can do better than that. Where did you think I was tonight, without Bailey here to keep me busy?"

She pursed her lips, the pucker a reminder of what he wanted to do to that mouth. Kissing her senseless was just the beginning of what he desired.

"I figured you were out on a *date*," she finally blurted out, the frown on her face as she said the word a dead giveaway to her thoughts on the matter.

He shook his head and laughed, relieved at her admission and the fact that she didn't like the idea of him with another woman.

She braced her hands on her hips, clearly annoyed. "What's so funny?"

Pushing himself to a standing position, he stepped closer. Her scent, the citrus aroma he'd come to associate with her, the same one his body automatically reacted to, wafted around him. "Oh, I don't know. Maybe the fact that you think I could be with another woman when I can't get that hot fucking kiss out of my head?"

Those same lips that were the object of his obsession parted in a surprised *oh*.

"Have you forgotten? Can you get it out of your
mind? Or do you lie in bed at night thinking about me
the way I do about you?"

Chapter Four

M IA HADN'T FORGOTTEN that kiss. Not for a second, and at the reminder, heat washed over her, tightening her skin. Austin's nearness didn't help.

He reached out and tucked a strand of her hair behind her ear, a gentle gesture that affected her like a sensual caress.

"I'm waiting for an answer."

She ran her tongue over her bottom lip. "No, I can't get it out of my head, either," she admitted.

"I thought so." He lifted her chin with his hand. "What are we going to do about this mutual wanting?"

"Nothing smart," she murmured.

He grazed her lip with the pad of his thumb, causing her to lean into him on a soft moan. She knew better than to give in. She'd spent the train ride home convincing herself to maintain the status quo, to steer clear. But how was she supposed to resist a man who worried about her welfare, who waited up for her to return, who looked at her as if he wanted to consume her?

"To hell with smart when it feels so good," he said.

She agreed. For the moment, she was finished fighting with herself, the devil on her shoulder winning. She'd deal with the repercussions later, and slid her tongue out to lick his finger, where it lingered on her mouth.

His gorgeous brown eyes darkened, and need pulsed through her veins, her sex damp with desire.

"Now let me taste that sweet mouth." He slipped a hand around the back of her neck and pulled her in. This time he didn't wait for her acquiescence. He dipped his head and covered her mouth with his.

The kiss was hot, his mouth branding her with the intensity of his need. He pulled her against him and she melted into his hard body. Her breasts crushed against his hard chest and her heart beat a mile a minute as he devoured her mouth, his tongue taking possession of hers.

He backed her up to the nearest wall, his lips never leaving hers. He grasped her waist, gliding his hand up her shirt, beneath the jacket, until he encountered her silk bra that he released in the front with a flick of his hand.

He tilted his head back, meeting her gaze, his irises dark with desire. "Take off the jacket," he said in a gruff voice. He backed up so she could do as he asked, and she leaned forward, shrugging off the leather and letting it fall to the floor.

He lifted her shirt up and over her head.

"Bra next."

She swallowed hard, and, emboldened by his need, she shrugged her shoulders, shimmying the opened garment down her arms so it fell on the floor. The cool air and his heated stare caused her nipples to pucker tightly.

"I wondered what these pretty tits looked like." He cupped her breasts in his hand, rubbing his thumbs over her distended nipples, the sensation causing a clenching of her core, an emptiness that needed to be filled.

She lifted her hands, intending to pull his shirt up so she could feel his skin. Turnabout was fair play, after all, but he shook his head.

"Don't. Not yet. Let me fulfill at least one of my personal fantasies first. I want to know what they taste like, too."

Before she could process his words, he dipped his head and covered one breast with his hot mouth, licking her flesh and teasing her nipples, grazing them, before he shocked her, sinking his teeth into her tender flesh.

She gasped at the bite of erotic pain that he quickly

soothed with gentle laps of his tongue. Pleasure swamped her, her legs trembling, her sex damp. She grasped his head, holding him tight as he continued to focus on her breasts, moving to the to the other side, giving her left breast the same sensual treatment.

By the time he was finished, her hips were shifting back and forth of their own accord, her body seeking fulfillment. He slid one strong thigh between her legs and soon she was writhing against him, waves of pleasure accosting her body. Her sex throbbed with desire and she whimpered aloud.

"I've got you," he said, wrapping an arm around her waist as his free hand unbuttoned her jeans and slid down her panties, his strong fingers gliding over her clit.

She moaned at the first touch of her most sensitive spot, falling back against his arm and the wall behind her.

"Let me make you feel good. Let me make you come."

She wasn't about to argue. Not when his fingers danced over her slick folds and his seductive words had her trembling, shaking, and on the verge of an explosive orgasm.

He picked up speed, his fingertip rubbing circles over her clit. He stroked her in just the right spot, in the most perfect way, and stars sparkled behind her eyes, warmth and pleasure sizzling along her nerve endings, the ultimate peak with reach. A tweak, a pinch, and she was calling his name, coming hard on and around his fingers. The waves rippled around her and she rode out the storm, pleasure consuming her.

He didn't let up, caressing her through her climax and as she came down from the high, and only when she was too sensitive to take his touch anymore did he slide his fingers out of her pants.

At the sudden loss, she forced her eyelids open and looked into his lust-filled gaze. "Austin," she whispered, her voice hoarse, in awe of what she'd just experienced at his hands.

"I like hearing my name on your lips when you come." A satisfied smile tugged at his lips.

"I like when you make me come." The admission caused her to blush.

Not breaking eye contact, he raised his fingers to his mouth and licked the taste of her off his fingers, causing a tug of renewed desire to flicker to life inside her. But her brain was just beginning to function again and though she couldn't say she regretted what just happened, she was pretty sure it hadn't been her smartest move. All the reasons she'd laid out to Amber returned, running through her brain on a never-ending loop. He was her boss, she loved her job, and ultimately they wanted very different things out of life and relationships.

She let out an unwitting sigh, wishing she could take it back the second the sound escaped her lips.

He met her gaze, eyeing her warily. "What's wrong?"

"Nothing," she said, and despite her reservations, she reached for the waistband of his pants, wanting to give him the same pleasure he'd bestowed on her.

He grabbed her wrist, gently pulling away, her hand grazing his hard erection, which strained against the taut fabric. "Fuck," he muttered, his voice sounding like rough gravel, his need obvious.

"Why are you stopping me?" she asked.

"Because it's clear I lost you."

She nodded because she couldn't deny the truth. "All the reasons this is a bad idea are shooting through my brain." She reached down and closed her jeans, feeling totally awkward, especially since she'd just come and he... hadn't.

"I get it," he said in an understanding tone. "I came on pretty strong when you walked in the door and I didn't give you time to think."

She sunk her teeth into her lower lip and shook her head. "I can make my own decisions and I own what happened between us. It wasn't you pushing me into anything. I just think since I work for you, we shouldn't get involved." She settled on the easiest explanation even though it hurt her to say it.

No reason for him to be privy to the fact that the future she envisioned for herself—a family and a man who loved her—were the things that would fill the emptiness she'd grown up with inside her. She always sugarcoated her time in foster care because she had had it better than most, but deep inside her she yearned for more. She didn't do casual relationships well and Austin was the whole package.

He could break her heart.

"I should go." She picked up her shirt, put it on, then turned and headed for her room, feeling his hot gaze on her back as she walked away.

★ ★ ★

AUSTIN WATCHED MIA leave before shutting the lights and heading upstairs to his room.

Alone.

He had to admit that hadn't been the outcome he'd envisioned when he'd had his hand down her pants, his fingers spreading her slick need over her clit as he made her come.

Her sigh had been his first clue something was wrong, and though she'd been willing to give him his turn, he didn't want her that way. He wanted her breathless and eager, no hesitation between them. Besides, he had the feeling she wasn't giving him the full reason for her reservations. Yes, she was his employee. Yes, it could be awkward and had bothered him, too, but he'd come to realize they had no one to answer to but themselves and she'd wanted him as much as he desired her. Something more was at play behind those expressive eyes of hers.

But unless he wanted something more than easy sex, he had no right to ask. So instead of her sexy lips wrapped around his dick or taking her upstairs to his bedroom, he was suffering from a painful case of blue balls he was going to have to deal with in the shower. And as he wrapped his soap-slickened hand around his cock, water streaming over him, it was Mia's mouth sucking him dry that took him over the edge and to completion.

He woke up the next morning and drove to pick up Bailey, bringing her home and going about his business as if the night hadn't occurred.

AUSTIN DROVE INTO work, pulling into the parking lot, early for the normal weekly meeting. A week had passed since that night he'd felt Mia's slick sex beneath his fingers and brought her to climax, his name on her lips, and he found the trip to the office a welcome reprieve from being alone in the house with Mia and pretending he didn't desire her with every breath he took.

He paused in the kitchen area and poured himself a cup of coffee when Jared Wilson joined him, leaning against the doorframe.

"Hey, man. How's it going?" Jared asked.

"Good. Keeping busy." Austin took a sip of the coffee, made in the Keurig machine that Dan splurged on for the team. "What about you?" he asked his friend.

"Same. Busy." He shrugged. "We miss you around the office, though I don't blame you for wanting more time at home with your daughter."

"It was the right choice."

"You don't miss the field work?" Jared asked.

Austin shook his head. "Surprisingly, no." His new work-from-home situation suited him fine.

"Austin?" Lara, the longtime receptionist at Alpha Security, looked past Jared, who moved aside to let her into the room. "You have a visitor," she said.

He narrowed his gaze. "I'm not expecting anyone. Who is it? An old client?"

She shook her head, concern etching her features. "She *says* she's your *wife*."

He flinched and cringed at the same time. Everyone here knew he was single and had had problems with his ex, so Kayla's attempted power play with Lara held no sway.

"Son of a bitch. I don't suppose you could tell her I'm not here?"

"I'd be more than happy to tangle with her if that's what you want," the ever-loyal Lara said. "But she's determined. I already told her you were busy and she said she would wait."

"Fine," he muttered. "Is the conference room cleared out?"

Lara nodded. "I'll bring her in there to wait."

"Everything okay?" Jared asked.

Austin slammed a frustrated hand against the counter. "The bitch showed up at my house demanding money or else she threatened to go after custody."

Jared let out a low whistle. "What'd you do?"

"Threw her out and called my attorney. My lawyer says we have a strong case based on Kayla's history, but we both know I have no proof of what a shitty mother she was. Aside from me and my parents, and we're all biased."

"Fuck."

Austin ran a hand through his hair. "You can say that again. I don't want to go through a legal battle or put Bailey through one, either. I don't trust Kayla not to bring my little girl into court just to push me against the wall. And there's no way in hell I'm paying her to go away. She'll just come back next time she runs out of cash again," he said, listing all the problems that kept him up nights. "I've been waiting for her next move. Guess this is it."

"Want backup when you face her?" Jared offered.

"Thanks but I can handle her." He hoped.

He left his coffee in the kitchen and headed to the conference room, where his ex was pacing back and forth behind the large table. She was dressed similarly to the last time he'd seen her, a tight dress, high heels, overdone makeup, and hair teased full. Compared to Mia's natural beauty, Kayla was plastic and fake, inside and out.

What had he seen in her the first time? It was too late to wonder now.

"Kayla," he said, stepping inside the room but leaving the door behind him open. "What are you doing here?" he asked, remaining on the far side of the conference table, away from his ex.

She met his gaze with a cool stare of her own. "I haven't heard from you and I've given you plenty of time to consider my offer."

He frowned at that. "It wasn't an offer, it was blackmail using your child as leverage. I told you I'm not paying you again. You received your settlement."

She let out a prolonged sigh. "Leave it to you to make this difficult." She pulled out a folded piece of paper from her purse. "This is notice of a hearing. I warned you I'd go for custody and I meant it."

"You bitch." Austin stared at the offending paper without touching it, rage filling him at the thought of Kayla getting anywhere near his daughter.

"Fine, don't take it." She slammed the sheet down onto the table. "It doesn't change the fact that you have to show up in court… Or you can pay me and this entire problem goes away. Poof. Just like that." She snapped her fingers in the air in a dismissive action.

The irony was she didn't want custody. She was counting on Austin caving into her demands out of fear she might win.

He curled his fingers into fists at his sides, breathing hard, trying to find a way to harness his anger. "In your eyes, Bailey's either a pawn in your bid for cash or a problem you don't want to deal with. That's how you see her, isn't it? Well, let me tell you something. You'll get my money or my daughter over my dead body."

"Promises, promises." She tossed her hair over her shoulder and treated him to a cool smile and walked out the door, leaving Austin… and the hearing notice behind.

★　★　★

MIA PUSHED THE shopping cart through the grocery store, filling up the wagon with all Bailey's and Austin's favorite foods, her mind occupied, as it often was, with thoughts of Austin.

In the days since she'd kissed him and he'd made her come apart beneath his hands, she fought the hard fight to put both things out of her mind. She tried not to pay attention to his finer qualities, either, but she couldn't help but notice his patience with his daughter, his dedication to his job, and his continued kindness toward Mia herself.

He'd never mentioned that night and if she hadn't caught him staring at her when he thought she wasn't looking, she'd think he had forgotten the incident completely. But the fact was, the sexual tension between them was thick, broken up only by the little girl Mia cared for.

She finished up her list, paid with the credit card Austin provided for house-related things, and headed to the SUV. She was engrossed with loading the bags into the trunk when someone pushed their cart into hers, shoving the metal end into the back bumper.

"Hey!" she said, glancing up to see a man she didn't recognize holding on to the handle of the cart that had hit her.

He stared at her, a scowl on his pock-marked face.

"Can I help you?" she asked, unnerved by both his actions and menacing expression.

He strode around the cart, getting into her personal space. She glanced around, unsure if there was anyone else around her. Afraid now, she began to tremble, gripping the cart harder in her hand. If he touched her, she'd scream loud enough to bring people inside the neighboring stores out here to help.

"I've got a message for you," he said, so close she could smell his bad breath. "Mind your own damned business and you'll be fine. Stick your nose where it doesn't belong and you'll have problems." He punctuated his message with a shove that didn't hurt her, just reinforced his point.

"What are you talking about?" she asked him.

"You look like a smart girl. Figure it out," he said, and took off without taking his cart with him.

Trembling, she put the last bag in the back of the truck, slid both carts into the collection area, and rushed to lock herself inside the SUV. She tried to think of what that threat meant and came up empty. She didn't know of anyone who'd want to threaten her, wasn't involved in anyone else's business. Not anymore.

The incident reminded her of the time before the trial of her former boss, when he'd sent someone to convince her that it was in her best interest to back off and not testify against him. But Parker Alexander was in jail and she was living a quiet life here. She bit down on her lower lip. It just didn't make any sense, but the incident had her rattled and she couldn't wait to get out of here.

The short drive home seemed endless. When she finally arrived at the house, she pulled the SUV into the garage and closed the door behind her before getting out of the car. The garage was big enough for her to still be able to open the trunk and unload the groceries, even with the electric door closed, and she felt safer now that she was back home. Austin's car was on his side of the garage and a sense of relief washed over her that she wasn't here alone.

She walked into the house, her arms loaded up with grocery bags, as many as she could carry hanging from each hand, and deposited them on the counter. She didn't see Austin, which meant he was in his office or the home gym, so she went about putting away the items she'd purchased.

When she finished that chore, she turned her attention to emptying the full dishwasher. She didn't realize how badly she was still shaking until she dropped a glass onto the floor. It shattered, the pieces spreading out around her.

"Dammit." She pulled out the garbage pail and dropped to her knees to pick up the larger pieces before she began sweeping up the rest.

She managed to place a few bigger shards into the trash, but when she lifted another, she missed how sharp and jagged the edges were and sliced her palm.

"Oww!" She dropped the glass and grabbed her hand only to find blood flowing from the cut.

She closed her eyes and groaned, doubting this day could get much worse.

"Mia?" Austin came up behind her. She hadn't noticed him entering the room. "I heard something shatter. Oh, shit," he said, taking in her bloodied hand.

She grasped her wrist and looked up at him. "I'm sorry. I was just trying to clean this up."

"You don't need to be sorry. Come here." He helped her up, lifting her beneath her elbow and walking her over to the sink. "Let me see." He gently turned her hand over but blood covered it, obscuring the cut.

"I can't believe I was so clumsy," she muttered.

He shook his head. "Don't worry about the glass. But we do have to see how deep the cut is." He turned on the faucet, sticking his finger underneath the running water to make certain it was cool. "Okay, this may hurt but let's see what we're dealing with. Ready?"

She drew a deep breath and nodded, letting him control things as they moved her hand beneath the spray. It was easy to see that the cut looked deep, and for all she knew, there were smaller shards of glass in the open wound.

"I think this is going to need stitches," he said,

reading her mind.

As soon as she took her palm away from the water, blood began to pool again.

"Let's head over to the emergency walk-in clinic," Austin said. "I think it'll be faster than dealing with the emergency room at the hospital."

She nodded.

He grabbed a clean hand towel from the drawer and pressed it against her hand. "Hold that there. I just need to put on shoes and grab my keys."

"You don't need to—"

He placed a hand beneath her chin and forced her to look at him. "Do not say I don't need to take you."

"Okay, but first call the Slaters and ask Tina if she can bring Bailey home with Robin for a playdate," Mia said of the next-door neighbor, who had a daughter one year younger than Mia. The girls often played together and they did each other favors when needed. "I have to pick her up in an hour and we won't make it in time. If Tina can't do it, I really can go alone." Not that she wanted to.

Austin's kind, caring demeanor calmed her nerves. She hated to admit it but she was glad he wanted to come with her. Taking an Uber by herself for stitches wasn't something she'd have looked forward to. She didn't do well with hospitals, needles, or blood.

He stared at her for so long she grew uncomfortable.

"What?" she asked. "What's wrong?"

He blinked, still gaping at her. "You thought of Bailey first," he said, looking at her with what looked like awed admiration.

"Of course I did."

"Right." He shook his head, as if clearing his thoughts. "It's just… after the day I had, you took me by surprise."

She wondered what he meant but she didn't have time to ask. "Austin? I need a fresh towel." Blood had soaked through the one she was using.

Hours and five stitches later, they returned home and Mia was forced to admit she'd needed Austin by her side. She was surrounded by unpleasant memories in the sterile, bland-colored hospital rooms to begin with. And she really didn't do well with pain.

He'd held her good hand, and when the doctor had injected around the cut to numb her skin, she'd tucked her head against his strong chest when the burning sensation became too much. She appreciated his strength and caring. He could have sent her in alone, not jumped up the minute she hesitated after they'd called her name.

He'd stopped to pick up dinner on the way home so she wouldn't have to worry about putting something together with one hand, which she would definitely have attempted to do, he'd cleaned up the broken glass mess in the kitchen, and he'd given Bailey her bath.

Although he'd instructed her to rest for the remainder of the night, she still wanted to help where she could. She changed into comfortable sweats and a tee shirt, and although the numbness had worn off, she was managing the throbbing sensation without too much trouble.

She walked upstairs to check and see if father or daughter needed anything before she turned in for the night. Voices sounded from Bailey's room and she paused outside the doorway.

"Daddy, you don't sound like a unicorn!" Bailey said, giggling.

"No? What do unicorns sound like?" Austin asked.

"Girls! Unicorns are girls."

The next sound was uncontrollable six-year-old giggling, obviously from being tickled. Just how did he think Bailey would relax enough to fall asleep if he worked her up right before bedtime? Tickles were tantamount to giving the little girl a sugar rush, Mia thought. She was about to walk into the room and tell him so when the voice of reason in her head stopped her.

It's not your place.

She wasn't Bailey's mother and Austin had given

her the night off. Who was she to walk in and tell him how to handle his own child? Sure, she might mention it in passing when they talked tomorrow, but for tonight she'd leave him and his daughter alone.

She was about to turn and leave the doorway when Austin lifted his head, catching sight of her, his dark gaze settling on hers, a warm smile on his face. Her stomach tumbled over at the sight.

"Wait for me downstairs?" he asked her in a sexy, gruff voice. "I want to talk to you."

She swallowed hard and nodded.

"Mia!" Bailey popped up from her prone position in bed.

Mia waved at her. "Night, Munchkin."

"Night, Mia," Bailey said, yawning big afterwards.

Austin encouraged Bailey to lie back down.

Maybe she'd fall asleep easily after all, Mia thought. She watched Austin pull the covers up and over Bailey's little shoulders before leaning down to kiss her good night.

Chapter Five

WHAT A FUCKING day today had been, Austin thought, finally getting Bailey down for the night. He hoped. Before he left her room for good, she'd asked for a glass of water, two other stuffed animals, and one more kiss good night. The last one especially hadn't been a hardship.

He headed back downstairs to talk to Mia, one, because he wanted to see how she was feeling, and two, he felt that as his daughter's caregiver, she needed to be read into what was going on with Bailey's mother.

He joined her in the family room, where she sat watching television, her injured hand resting in her lap, and settled into the cushion beside her.

"How's the pain?" he asked.

"I'm okay. Ibuprofen is covering it for the most part." She glanced at him through lowered lids. "Thank you for taking me to the hospital today… and staying with me while they stitched me up. I'm not a big fan of hospitals. Bad memories and all that." She treated him to a sad smile.

"Care to share?" He was curious about Mia, her past and what made her tick.

She sighed. "My mom died of cancer. I was an only child and I spent a lot of time in hospitals until she passed away. Needles, IVs, the antiseptic smell…" She curled a leg beneath her on the sofa. "I'm squeamish and I hate pain, but I was already worked up before the doctor took out the injection to numb me."

And after the awful hospital stays with her mom, she'd gone to foster care, he thought, a little girl left alone, without a relative in the world to love her. Pain filled him at the thought.

He managed a smile so she wouldn't think he was pitying her. She was a proud, strong woman and wouldn't appreciate the sentiment. "I think you handled the whole thing pretty well. Except for the part when you shook in my arms. But I liked being there for you, so it's all good." He tried to make light of the situation.

She laughed, which had been his goal.

"I am sorry about your mom," he said, not wanting to be callous and ignore what she'd confided in him.

"Thanks. It's funny, the things I remember and

those I don't. I remember what my mom looked like, I think… but not what she smelled like. But I remember the scent and look of the hospital she died in." Mia shrugged, obviously used to living with the past. "Who knows how memory works."

"I wish I knew the answer to that," he said, his tone so deadly serious she jerked her head up to meet his gaze.

"Why?"

He blew out a long breath, wanting to have this conversation, as much for himself as for his daughter. He needed to talk to someone, and both his gut and his heart told him *this woman* would help him and understand. "Bailey was four when her mother left and I don't know what she remembers. Does she recall her mom flinging her around by her arm? Hurting her? Leaving bruises?" He winced at the thought, his protectiveness rising as it always did when it came to his daughter.

"Oh, Austin." Mia placed a hand on his shoulder, her touch both arousing and soothing at the same time. "That has to be so hard for you to wonder."

He nodded. "It is. And Kayla showed up at my office earlier today." Just the memory of seeing her, of her smug attitude and lack of caring about their daughter, had him seething all over again.

As if sensing his reaction, she began to massage his

shoulder where she touched him, working the muscles with her one good hand.

Her touch was electric, the desire to do more than talk filling him, but the situation needed to be explained.

"What did she want?" Mia asked.

"She handed me a notice of a custody hearing," he said through clenched teeth. "It was her big shot. She wanted me to know she's not above taking this all the way if I don't pay her off beforehand."

Mia shook her head, her expression one of horror. He agreed. He didn't know how any mother could bargain over a child.

"No wonder you're upset. There has to be something you can do." Mia looked at him with all the faith in the world.

Faith he desperately needed to believe in. "I hired a private investigator to look into her life. Top to bottom, from her finances to her personal life, her contacts, friends, men she hangs around with. You name it. I don't care how intrusive, I want everything he can dig up."

Mia nodded her approval. "Good. I'm sure if she's willing to play dirty with you, she's not squeaky-clean in her personal life."

"That's my hope. But all this just sucks. Because it comes back to what Bailey remembers. If she does recall what her mom did to her, my custody situation would be that much stronger... assuming a court would rely on the memory of a small child." He pinched the bridge of his nose, a headache forming at his next thought. "But what kind of shitty father... am I to even want her to recall that just because it'll help me to keep her?"

Mia leaned onto her knees and scooted closer to him, the warmth of her body a much-needed balm to his senses. "You're the best father I know. Seriously. Bailey is the luckiest little girl in the world. Don't ever doubt it," she said, reassuring him.

"You have no idea what it means to hear that." He paused, thinking about what possible plans his ex could have in the future. He didn't put it past her to act underhandedly. "I want you to be careful when you're out, especially with Bailey, and if you see Kayla or she tries to approach Bailey, I need to know about it immediately."

A flicker of uncertainty crossed Mia's face. "Umm..." Her voice trailed off, her tone concerned.

"Mia? What's wrong?"

She swiped her tongue over lips in a definite nervous gesture. "This afternoon, I was grocery shopping and a stranger approached me. He said something really odd and I couldn't figure out what he meant, but now that you said Bailey's mother is playing dirty, I can't help but wonder if she had anything to do with it."

Austin stiffened. "What happened? And don't leave anything out."

"Okay." She raised her gaze to meet his. "So I was putting the bags into the car and someone slammed their cart against mine. I looked up and there was a man standing there."

"You've never seen him before?"

She shook her head. "He walked around the cart and got really close to me. He said…" She closed her eyes, as if trying to remember the words exactly.

She opened them again. "He said, 'Mind your own damned business and you'll be fine. Stick your nose where it doesn't belong and you'll have problems.' Then he shoved me. I asked what he was talking about. And he just said I looked like a smart girl and to figure it out. And then he walked away."

His hands curled into fists at the thought of any-one laying a hand on Mia, threatening her, scaring her in any way. He thought back to this afternoon. She'd come home from the store and he'd heard a crash, run downstairs, and found her on the floor surrounded by broken glass.

He shook his head, understanding now. "You were shaken up and you dropped the glass. That son of a bitch really frightened you."

She glanced up at him with wide eyes and nodded. "It reminded me of when I had to testify against my old employer. He tried to threaten and bully me into keeping quiet."

"But you didn't," he said, proud of her for standing her ground.

That was one of the reasons he'd hired her. Instead of her past scaring him off, he felt the opposite way. In his job as a bodyguard, he knew how hard it was for a person to show up in court and send someone else to jail. He'd seen people run instead of standing their ground. He'd felt that if Mia was strong enough to testify against her wealthy former employer, she had good moral character and she was someone he'd want around his daughter.

"Do you think your ex-wife hired someone to scare me away?" Mia asked.

He doubted she realized it but her hand was still on his shoulder, stroking him through his shirt. And though he wanted to answer her, her caress felt too good, making it difficult to concentrate. His body was beginning to respond to her nearness and her fruity, sweet scent. His cock was hard and it was all he could do not to draw her into his arms, devour her mouth, and work his way down her body, tasting every luscious inch of her.

"Come here," he said instead of replying. Unable

to help himself, he opened his arms. He told himself he was offering comfort from her earlier fright, that he needed the same consolation from her.

He was lying. He just plain wanted her. But the choice whether to come to him was hers. It always would be.

★   ★   ★

MIA LOOKED AT the handsome, sexy man beckoning her to him with open arms. She'd walked away once before and she wasn't sure she had the strength to do it again. She glanced down at his hand before placing her smaller, uninjured palm against his.

Skin brushed skin. An electric pulse danced up her arm, traveled through her body to her breasts, hardening her nipples and thudding through her swollen sex.

"Is this wrong?" she asked him, meeting his heavy-lidded gaze.

"Only if we think it is." He reached up and tucked a strand of hair behind her ear, his fingers gentle as they slid over her cheek, the featherlight touch arousing her even more.

She leaned into him, his masculine scent going to her head. "It feels like a cliché to say this but how can it be wrong if it feels so good?" And it did. Her entire body was buzzing with need.

His hand drifted to cup her jaw. Tipping her head,

he brushed his lips over hers. At the first touch of his mouth, all her concerns fled in the wake of his potent masculine need. He held her chin in his hand and kissed her, his tongue passing through her lips and tangling with hers.

Heat cascaded through her and she needed more. More of his hot mouth taking her, dominating her lips, and just more of him. She climbed into his lap, straddling him, settling her knees on either side of his thighs, and grinding her sex against his hard erection. She couldn't get close enough fast enough, the barrier of clothing between them driving her insane.

His cock was thick and she needed to touch him, to feel his skin against her hand. She pulled at the drawstring on his athletic pants in an attempt to do just that, but the movement hurt her stitches, causing her to wince and moan under his mouth.

"You're going to hurt yourself." He grasped her wrist, pulling her hand against her side. "Let me do the work," he said in a gruff, sexy voice.

"If you insist." She knew anything he did would make her feel good. "But let's take this to a bedroom. I don't want to get caught," she said.

"Good idea. Your place or mine?" he asked with a sexy wink.

She laughed at his playfulness. "Your call." She didn't know which made more sense or wouldn't her haunt more later. If he chose her room, she'd have memories of him in her bed. If he chose his, it would feel too intimate.

"I've got a secure lock," he said, grasping her good hand and leading her out of the family room, up the stairs, and to his bedroom, shutting the door behind him.

She wanted time to catalogue things about the man, his taste in furniture, and the personal effects sitting around. Although she straightened up after herself and Bailey, he had a cleaning service do a more thorough job once a week. She'd never had a reason to come into his personal domain. But no sooner had he turned the lock on the door than he picked her up and laid her on the bed, his big body coming down on hers, and all thoughts of anything but his hard muscles and warm breath against her skin were gone in an instant.

"I've been going crazy, lying in this bed, imagining you right downstairs, wondering if you sleep in sexy lingerie or a simple tee shirt with your gorgeous breasts peeking through." He slid her shirt up and over her head and tossed it to the floor.

She wore a flimsy bra, just enough to be appropriate walking through the house, and he moved the cups aside, allowing her breasts to show above, pushed together by the stretch of fabric against her full mounds.

"So fucking perfect." He bent his head and pulled one nipple into his mouth, tugging with his teeth until the same sensations shot straight to her core.

Her panties were already damp, and she writhed beneath him, seeking friction and harder contact he was only too happy to give. His hard cock ground against her sex while he played and toyed with her breasts and nipples, alternating between each, long, loving laps of his tongue and short bites with his teeth that had her hips bucking beneath him.

She wrapped her arms around his waist, digging the fingernails of her good hand into his ass, holding him tight as she strained against him.

He pushed himself upright to a sitting position, grasping her arms and placing them over her head. "You seem to forget I'm the one doing the work. Which means I'm the one in charge." His eyes gleamed with determination and a heady, sexy fire, his demanding tone arousing her even more. "I want to make sure you don't hurt your hand. Besides, I want to make you feel good."

He flicked open the front clasp of her bra and helped her writhe out of the garment before turning his attention to the sweat pants. He tugged on the white drawstring and pulled the pants loose, then moved aside and stripped her, removing her panties along with the sweats.

She was naked and splayed out on his bed, a feast if he wanted to indulge. And when he grasped her hips and slid downward, his face within inches of her pussy, she knew that he did. He slid his tongue over her sex and she moaned aloud, then immediately realized she couldn't risk Bailey hearing her. It wasn't easy to keep quiet when he didn't let up, sucking, licking, and devouring her like a starving man.

She lost any inhibitions to the sensations he caused, lifting her hips and grinding into his mouth, pleasure overtaking her. Wave after wave of pleasure bringing her higher and closer to climax.

He slipped one finger inside her, finding the exact spot that had her thighs shaking, her muscles quivering, and she clenched her inner walls around him.

"Hot, wet, and tight. Fuck," he muttered, raising his head and sliding his thumb over her clit.

"Oh, damn, that feels good." She bucked at his talented touch. "So good," she moaned, trying to keep her voice low.

And when he pressed down harder, she exploded, coming hard against his touch, soaring higher as he pumped his finger in and out of her, hitting her G-spot each time, causing exquisite pressure and pleasure as she rode out her release.

She was still quivering when he stood beside the

bed and stripped off his clothes, her gaze gliding over his muscular body, perfectly ripped from working out, and then lower to his thick, hard, clearly aroused cock.

He pulled open his nightstand and retrieved a condom, ripping it open and gliding it on. Her sex throbbed at the sight, arousal consuming her. He rejoined her on the bed, his big body looming over hers.

"Ready to come again?" he asked her, grasping his erection in his hand and deliberately gliding his thickness over her wet, aching sex.

She groaned at the feel of him sliding over her clit, hard and hot. "Ready, willing, and able," she assured him, her body definitely soft for him.

He braced a hand on either side of her shoulders and the head of his cock settled at her entrance. His gaze locked on hers, dark and slumberous, desire oozing from him as he pushed himself into her. She trembled, her slick body accepting him easily, as she adjusted to his thickness.

"Bend your legs," he said, and she did as he asked, the new position causing him to glide deeper still.

"Austin." She groaned, and as if the sound of his name released the hold he'd kept on himself, he began to thrust into her, taking her hard, his hips pounding against her.

She hadn't been kidding when she said she was

ready, willing, and able. Her body began the climb the minute he withdrew and took her over and over, his steady thrusts a perfect counterpoint to the spot he hit inside her. The same one he'd found earlier with his finger.

She took in his expression, jaw tight, sweat dripping from his temple, his concentration completely on her face. She felt owned by him, his body reading hers well, his focus on her complete.

"You're going to come first," he said, swiping his tongue over her lips. He pumped into her over and over, and she barely recognized the incoherent sounds ripping from her throat as pleasure consumed her.

"Yes, yes. I'm coming," she said, her body giving him what he demanded, glorious waves consuming her.

He took her release as a sign and let go, allowing her orgasm to trigger his own. "Fuck, Mia. So damn good." He thrust over and over until he'd expended himself and collapsed on top of her, his body deliciously warm and slick with sweat.

At some point she'd wrapped her arms around his neck and now she held on, taking these few precious moments, when he couldn't see her face or how much he'd affected her, to come back to herself.

As she breathed in and out, regaining her composure, she released him, hoping he'd take the hint and roll off her. She wasn't going to regret what they'd done but she couldn't act like it was anything more than it was. Great sex with her hot employer that didn't change the facts.

She worked for him and nothing could come of this fling. Never mind that he represented everything she'd want in her life if only things could be different. If he were the type of man to want more.

★ ★ ★

AUSTIN ROLLED OFF Mia, his body still buzzing from the best fucking orgasm ever. He headed for the bathroom to dispose of the condom. His brain, which had shut off during his release, clicked back on as he lay on top of her, feeling the softness of her skin, her breath heavy on his neck.

He'd had plenty of sex in his lifetime, although not much lately, and what he'd shared with Mia was more. More explosive, more in tune with his feelings… more everything. And though he'd wondered briefly what the fuck he'd done—he never brought a woman home to the house where he lived with his daughter, let alone contemplated sex in the bedroom with his kid a room over—he didn't think he could bring himself to regret that it had happened with Mia.

He returned to the bed, where she was retrieving her clothes from the floor. He took in her nakedness, her skin flushed, her hair tousled, and his cock jerked, awake again.

"Rushing out?" he asked, sliding back onto the mattress.

She glanced over her shoulder, those big green eyes looking back at him warily. "It seems like the right... the smart thing to do."

Before *he* asked *her* to leave? Was that thought going through her mind? No, that hadn't been in his plan. "I still don't think it was a mistake," he told her.

She sat back down beside him, clutching her clothes to her chest. "No, I don't think it was a mistake, either."

Well, thank God for that, he thought. One hurdle he didn't have to climb... talking her down from panic.

"I'm just not sure we should repeat it though."

He didn't question why not. All the reasons they'd tried to avoid the inevitable still existed. No reason to list them all again. But having experienced sex with Mia, he had no doubt there would be a repeat. She just needed convincing.

He reached out and hooked an arm around her waist, pulling her toward him. She released her hold on the clothes in her hand and let him settle her on top of him.

"Austin—"

"Mia," he parroted, his face inches from hers. "You're not going anywhere until we get a few things straight."

Her lips fought a smile. "And what would those things be?" she asked, shifting her body into his, getting more comfortable... just as he was growing harder.

Before he could act on what his body demanded, they needed to be in accord. "We already agree we don't regret it but apparently we don't agree on what happens next. From my point of view, we have to be discreet around Bailey but there's no reason this has to be a one-night-only thing."

She sighed. "I can't think of anything dumber than for me to allow this to continue."

He did his best not to wince at her stark statement. "Because?"

Her gaze met his, softness and caring in those depths. "You're charming, you're a good man, and you're an even better father. Not to mention you're spectacular in bed. But you're also my employer."

"She says while sprawled naked on top of me." He ran a hand over the back of her head, tangling his fingers through her hair, and she purred like a contented kitten. "Stop thinking so hard and just enjoy." And in case she needed convincing, he slid his tongue across her lips, licking back and forth until she parted her mouth, giving in on a soft moan. "And now we're in agreement," he said before diving in and taking full advantage.

His tongue dueled with hers, his fingers digging into her hips as she ground her sex against his aching dick. This wasn't about slow and fast. Not when he was inches from her sweet pussy and one wrong roll would push him inside her.

He lifted his head and ground out, "Condom. Top drawer."

She leaned over and found a packet. Ripping it open, she sat back and lowered the covering over his cock, her hands trembling with the same need coursing through him.

"This time you're going to ride me," he told her.

Her eyes grew hazy with desire and she lifted herself onto her knees and took his cock in hand. Next thing he knew, she was slowly lowering herself onto him, accepting his thickness into her slick body. She clasped him in heat and he nearly came right there.

He held on, though, needing her to come first. Always. He gritted his teeth as she began to move, gliding up and down, milking him for all he was worth. He grasped her hips, holding on and grinding her onto him with each downward pass.

She began to make those sexy noises that told him she was close, so he slipped his finger over her clit and she shuddered, her inner walls contracting around him as she came on a low moan of pleasure. His balls tightened, drew up, and just as before, her climax triggered his.

He slammed up and into her, taking her hard and fast. She called out his name, a second orgasm crashing over her as he spilled himself into her.

She fell over him, her body giving way, and she breathed heavily into his ear. He held on to her, not ready to let go. But this time, after his trip to the bathroom, when he found her getting dressed, he forced himself not to ask her to stay. He had Bailey to think about, the center of his life, who would not understand her daddy in bed with her nanny. Who didn't deserve to be confused by grown-up complications.

He let Mia slip away quietly, walking away without conversation or discussion, knowing that though he might sleep with her, he couldn't ever let himself get attached. The good thing was, she obviously felt the same way. What he didn't understand was why that thought bothered him so damned much.

Chapter Six

MIA WAITED FOR Bailey to get out of school. She'd gotten to the parking lot early so she could get a decent parking spot and decided to wait in the car until it was almost time for the kids to be let out. She listened to music on the radio, her mind continually drifting back to her night with Austin.

Even when she wasn't thinking about him, her body still hummed with desire. He'd lit a fire in her she hadn't known existed. And though the next day they'd both acted like nothing happened, she knew better.

So did he.

Over the last week, his gaze tracked hers when he thought she wasn't looking, and she was just as guilty, her gaze falling on him over Bailey's head. If he turned around, she watched his tight, sexy ass. If he looked her way, she met his knowing stare. Sunday night, she stayed locked in her room, not even coming out for her normal cup of tea. She didn't want to fall into a nightly routine that could be detrimental to her heart and her peace of mind. Because Austin was a man she could easily fall for.

Unwilling to think about it any longer, she climbed out of the car to wait for Bailey by the exit to the school. She smiled at a few of the friendlier moms, and soon the bell rang and the kids began to flow out, the teachers of the younger children walking them to the doors.

Mia caught sight of Bailey's dark hair and was just about to call the girl's name when someone did it first.

"Bailey!"

Mia spun around in time to see the child's mother waving toward her. "No." Mia pushed past a few parents to reach Bailey first, grasping her hand just as Kayla strode into their personal space.

"Bailey, baby, it's Mommy!"

Mia froze, holding Bailey's hand tight. This was what Austin feared, Bailey being confronted by her mother, and neither Mia nor Austin knew what the little girl remembered about her.

Bailey squeezed Mia's fingers back, her little hand feeling fragile in Mia's larger one.

"Bailey?"

"You need to leave," Mia said to Kayla, keeping her voice level so as not to frighten Bailey even more.

Kayla looked nothing like the other moms in jeans,

shirts, and jackets. Instead she wore a skimpy dress and high heels, as out of place in this environment as she was in her daughter's life.

"I have a right to see my child."

"Not according to the custody agreement I understand exists."

Kayla perched her sunglasses on top of her head, her eyes not focused on Bailey but glaring at Mia. "Bailey, honey? Don't you remember me?" She wasn't even smart enough to drop down to Bailey's level to try and reach her.

Bailey backed her body into Mia's, causing Kayla to frown as her daughter clearly made her choice. A choice no child should have to make, between a caregiver and her mother.

"Kayla, go now."

"Is there a problem?" One of the teachers strode over and asked.

"Yes," Mia said.

"No," Kayla replied.

Mia glanced at the older woman. "I'm allowed to pick up Bailey. She isn't." She gestured to Kayla, refusing to call her Bailey's mother out loud. She didn't deserve the acknowledgment and she refused to scare the little girl.

"I'm sorry, Ms....?" She glanced at Kayla for an answer.

"Gibson. Kayla Gibson," she said sullenly.

"Ms. Gibson, do I need to go to the office and check the parental forms?" *Or will you leave quietly?* The words were implied.

Mia, keeping her grasp on Bailey and brushing her head soothingly, held her breath.

"I'll go." Kayla plopped her sunglasses back down on her nose. "But this isn't the end of things. You"— she pointed at Mia, almost poking at her with her finger—"tell my ex-husband he knows what he has to do if he wants this to end."

She glanced at Bailey, almost as an afterthought. "I'll see you soon," she said, waving her fingers at her daughter... for show. There was no caring that Mia could see.

She waited until Kayla not only walked away but climbed into her car and drove off before taking Bailey and walking her to a quiet space on the grass.

Mia knelt down and glanced at the little girl, who looked up at her with big, frightened eyes. "Are you okay?" Mia asked her.

"I don't like her," Bailey whispered. "She yells a lot."

Mia swallowed hard. She'd minored in psychology but nothing had prepared her for this. "You know her?" Better than saying *do you remember her?* Mia didn't know if it made a difference.

"That's Mommy," Bailey whispered. "She hurt me."

Oh, shit. That was the perfect answer to Austin's custody problem and the worst answer for this happy little girl.

"Don't worry. She won't ever hurt you again." Mia kissed her cheek and took her hand. "Let's go see Daddy," she suggested, knowing she was out of her depth.

They drove home in silence, which was unusual for Bailey on any normal day, but today wasn't a typical day.

Austin was waiting for them in the kitchen when they entered the house, downing a sports drink. He'd obviously just worked out and had timed his ending to see his daughter when she arrived home from school.

"Bailey Button!" he called out.

Bailey trudged inside, dumping her backpack in the hallway. She didn't call out *Daddy!* the way she usually did and she didn't jump into his arms.

"Mia?" he asked, obviously concerned.

She bit down on her lower lip. "Umm… Bailey, go get a juice box from the fridge, okay? I want to talk to your dad."

The little girl shuffled away and Mia's heart broke a little more.

"What happened?" Austin bit out.

"Bailey had a visitor outside school." She quickly recounted the incident with Kayla, including Bailey's reaction of curling into Mia and her admission that she remembered the woman as her mommy, and as someone who not only yelled a lot but who'd hurt her.

"Son of a bitch!" Austin's hands curled into fists and Mia immediately reached out to soothe him. She grasped his tight hand and urged him to relax, rubbing her thumb over his straining knuckles. "Bailey can't see you like this," she whispered, reminding him that his focus needed to be on his daughter.

He met her gaze, his dark and solemn and grateful, and he nodded. "I'll go talk to her."

"I'll give you time alone." Mia reluctantly released her grasp on him and stepped aside so he could speak to his daughter.

"Mia, stay. Please. Bailey needs you." He paused. "*I* need you," he said, the words obviously not easy for him to admit out loud.

How could she say no to him? Why would she want to? He didn't know, but being needed was her Achilles heel and being needed by Austin? She'd be there for him, for whatever he needed.

"Of course."

He drew in a deep breath, clearly tamping down on his rage, pushing it somewhere his daughter couldn't see or feel as he joined her at the table, where she played with her juice box straw, not drinking.

Mia lingered in the background, sticking close but not wanting to intrude.

"Hey." He settled into the chair next to Bailey, looking at the little girl who was so obviously his whole world. "Mia told me you saw your mom today."

Bailey swung her legs back and forth beneath her but didn't answer.

"She said you remember her?" Austin continued, his tone gentle.

She tipped her little chin up and down. "She scares me," she whispered.

And wasn't that an awful thing for her to live with and think about her mother, no matter how deserving, Mia thought.

Austin smoothed a hand over the back of her head. "That's okay, baby girl." He pulled her into a tight embrace.

Mia admired him for how well he was handling this situation and his daughter's pain.

Bailey, however, remained silent.

"Believe me?" he asked.

"Yes, Daddy."

He sighed at her soft, defeated attitude.

Mia knew, for both their sakes, Bailey needed to put today's episode out of her mind and let her father shoulder the burden, but she was too young to understand.

"So I was thinking," Austin said. "What if you, me, and Mia went for pizza and ice cream for dinner?"

Mia's heart beat a little faster at how easily he included her in the outing, chiding herself at the same time for thinking it meant any more than doing her job as Bailey's nanny. Blurring the lines by sleeping with Austin was not going to be easy.

At the mention of pizza, or more likely ice cream, a little smile finally curved Bailey's lips. "With sprinkles?" she asked.

"Lots and lots of colored sprinkles."

Mia grinned. He obviously didn't care how big the sugar rush or how late Bailey's bedtime ended up being because of it. He just wanted his daughter to be happy.

And Mia fell a little harder for Austin because of it.

TOMORROW WAS NATIONAL Chocolate Cupcake Day, so Bailey and Mia were in the kitchen baking enough cupcakes for the class, because, of course, Bailey had volunteered for cupcake duty. As Austin walked to the kitchen, he listened to his daughter's chatter and Mia's laughter and something inside him eased.

These last few days he'd been a ball of stress. He'd just gotten off the phone with the private investigator who was looking into his ex-wife. So far he hadn't found any dirt on Kayla but she did have a man in her life, and Austin told the investigator to put his focus there. The good news was she hadn't returned to cause trouble or bother Bailey. He had no doubt her first attempt outside the school was a warning to Austin because Kayla wanted cold, hard cash. He wouldn't put it past her to try something else to upset Bailey and piss him off in her quest to get him to buy her off.

They both knew the court date loomed at the end of the year and something had to give before then. He was counting on the PI to find something incriminating on Kayla, because Austin wasn't going to put his daughter through any more stress by being forced to relive past events. She was going through enough, courtesy of her mother.

The night after she'd seen Kayla, Bailey began having nightmares. She'd wake up crying, coming to him and disrupting his eight hours because it took her too long to fall back to sleep... in his bed.

With Bailey's life in turmoil, Mia stepped up even more. She kept Bailey's schedule busy with friends and special projects so she had no time to dwell on the mean lady at school, as she'd called Kayla one night while crying herself to sleep and breaking Austin's heart.

Mia fit into his life so seamlessly and on so many

levels it scared him, and for a man who used to use a gun in his daily job, that struck him as ridiculous. But look at the situation he was in thanks to letting himself be manipulated by Bailey's mother. Austin was finished with marriage and happily ever after and Mia still wanted those things. Hell, after the childhood she'd had, she deserved those and more.

He just couldn't give them to her. With a little girl in his room at night and them both keeping busy during the day, he and Mia hadn't connected again, and maybe not being able to drag her back into his bed really was for the best.

"Can I lick the bowl?" Bailey's voice traveled to him and he forced himself to stop overthinking and step into the room.

"Hi, girls." Austin came up to the counter. Mia was putting the cupcakes into the oven while Bailey was, as she'd requested, running her fingers through the bowl and feasting on the remaining batter.

"Daddy!"

"Those cupcakes look good," he said as Mia slid the final tin into the oven.

She turned back to him and grinned. "It's Bailey approved. Chocolate cupcake and confetti frosting."

"Yum." He actually wasn't so sure about the confetti. He figured it was too rich for his taste.

"Taste." Bailey held out a finger for him to lick,

but it was a wet finger that had been in her mouth numerous times. "Umm, I think I'll take a pass."

Mia chuckled. She picked a clean part of the bowl that Bailey hadn't yet tackled and swiped her finger into the batter. She slid it into her mouth and moaned in delight, inadvertently meeting Austin's gaze as her lips cupped the frosting-coated finger.

His cock twitched at the sexy sound that escaped her lips, not to mention the visual of her sucking off her finger, something she'd yet to do to him. He was grateful the counter between them blocked his firm package from being noticed. Her gaze locked on his, sudden awareness in the mossy depths. He wanted nothing more than to say to hell with what was for the best and drag her off to his bedroom so she could suck on his cock the same way.

"Isn't it good?" Bailey asked Mia.

She jerked her stare away from Austin and he swallowed a rough cough.

"I think your friends are going to love the cupcakes," Mia said in a husky voice. "Let me set a timer." She turned away to focus on her task but the awareness between them remained.

★ ★ ★

AFTER DROPPING THE cupcakes off at Bailey's school, Mia returned home to a blue car turning into the driveway. Since it was blocking her ability to pull into the garage, she parked on the street and exited the vehicle, walking toward the car.

A man climbed out of the driver's side and met her halfway down the drive. "Mia Atwood?" he asked.

She didn't recognize him at all, which made her nervous, especially after what had happened at the grocery store.

"You've been served," he said, handing her the manila envelope she hadn't noticed was in his hand.

"What is this?" she asked.

"Information's inside. Have a good day."

"But—"

He didn't wait for her to speak, merely returned to his car, climbed in, and turned on the ignition. She stepped aside so he could pull out of the driveway, turning her attention to the ominous-looking envelope.

Could this have to do with Austin's custody case? She opened the folded flap and pulled out the blue-backed page, scanning the contents, a sickening feeling settling in the pit of her stomach with every word she read.

The State of New York versus Parker Alexander. Retrial for embezzlement among other crimes. She swallowed hard, nausea filling her. She didn't understand, thought her ex-employer was in jail. She flipped the envelope in her hand and a business card fell out. A glance told her it was the same district attorney she'd dealt with during the last trial.

She headed inside, glad Austin was at his weekly meeting in the office. She didn't need him to see her shaken up before she had all the details.

A quick call to Kate Collins, the district attorney, answered her questions and she didn't like what she learned. Parker had been released from jail when his conviction was overturned due to a technicality the DA didn't bother to explain and Mia really didn't care why. The end result was the same. He was out and the state was retrying him. Because she'd moved to Connecticut and there had been no reason for her to leave a forwarding address, as the case had been concluded, it had taken Kate time to find Mia and let her know she'd be needed at another trial.

She was *not* happy.

She didn't want her life, her job, or Austin and Bailey's life disrupted by her having to go to New York to testify.

She sighed and was about to head to her room when the home telephone rang. She answered. "Rhodes residence."

"Hello, is Mr. Rhodes home?" an efficient female voice asked.

"No, can I take a message?" Mia tucked the phone

between her ear and shoulder and grabbed a piece of paper and pen.

"It's the Lakewood Elementary school."

"This is Mia Atwood, Bailey's nanny. Is everything okay?"

"Oh, Ms. Atwood. I see you're on the approved list to pick up Bailey. We seem to have an issue. There's a woman here claiming to be Bailey's mother and she's insisting she see her daughter. She wants to remove her from the premises but she's not on our list."

"No, she isn't. I'll call Mr. Rhodes immediately. Please don't let her anywhere near Bailey," Mia said. "I'll come by myself to pick her up when school is over."

"The problem is, the children were in the hallway walking to the gym and Bailey saw Ms. Gibson. We took Bailey away and brought her to the nurse's office but Ms. Gibson is still here and making a scene," the other woman explained, sounding upset now that she'd gotten into the details.

Mia's stomach flipped over. "I'll call Mr. Rhodes immediately. Please don't let her near Bailey," she repeated urgently.

Mia hung up the phone, grabbed her cell phone in one hand and her keys in another. She set the house alarm and called Austin's cell phone as she ran for the car, which she'd left in the street, thinking only of getting to the school and to Bailey as quickly as possible.

He picked up on the second ring. "Mia? What's wrong?" he asked, probably because she never called him unless Bailey was sick.

"Your ex is at Bailey's school." She detailed the rest of the situation. "I'm heading over now."

Austin swore. "Okay, I'll meet you there. I'm already on my way home, so it shouldn't take long. You know what to do. Keep her away from my baby."

Mia swallowed hard. She knew. "You got it," she promised as she reached her car.

The school wasn't far from the house and Mia reached it in record time, bypassing yellow lights that turned red as she drove past.

Mia arrived at the school, stopping at the main office to sign in. She didn't see Kayla and she didn't ask where she was. "Where's Bailey? Is she still at the nurse's office?"

The gray-haired woman behind the desk in the office nodded. "I thought it would be best to put her someplace where she couldn't see her mother since what she said seemed to upset her so much."

Mia swallowed hard. "Where is it?"

"Down the hall to the left," the other woman said.

Mia ran, slowing when she reached the nurse's office, not wanting to freak Bailey out. She stepped into the room and smiled at the school nurse. "I'm here for Bailey?"

"Mia!" The little girl flew out from a side room and wrapped her arms around Mia, holding on tight.

"Hey, baby." Mia glanced over her head to meet the nurse's kind gaze. "Is she okay?"

"A little shaken up. She stopped crying when I gave her juice and a book to read so she'd put the incident out of her mind. I just thought it was best she went home early to her family."

Mia stroked the child's head. "Her father will be with her in a little while," she assured the nurse. "Ready to go home?"

Bailey nodded against her.

"Do you need to get anything from your classroom first?"

"No." She stepped back and glanced up at Mia. Tears stained her cheeks and Mia's heart squeezed tight in her chest.

Unfortunately, to leave the school, they had to walk past the main office. If luck held, they wouldn't run into Kayla. Mia led Bailey down the hall and turned toward the office. She immediately caught sight of Austin, having his say with the principal and the office staff, no doubt making it clear Kayla was not allowed anywhere near his child and only Austin, Mia, and Austin's parents were allowed into the school or to pick up Bailey.

"Daddy!"

Austin turned and Bailey ran into his open arms. He picked her up and held her tight against him. "Do we have an understanding?" he asked Principal Shay, a middle-aged man with a good reputation among teachers and parents.

"Of course. And we have your instructions in writing. Don't worry."

Austin nodded. He glanced at Mia. "I'm getting a restraining order," he muttered. "Are we ready to go?"

She nodded. "I'll meet you and Bailey at home."

"I want to ride with Mia." Bailey wriggled to get down from her father's arms.

"Honey, no. I'm sure your dad wants to talk to you."

"It's fine," Austin said, an unreadable glint in his eye. But she didn't get the sense he was unhappy about his daughter's proclamation.

Mia made sure Bailey was buckled into her car seat and they headed home. The adrenaline of her day was beginning to wear off and she was exhausted. She hoped Bailey would be in a let's-just-chill-and-watch-a-movie mood. All Mia wanted to do was relax.

But when they arrived at the house, the burglar alarm was going off and the police were parked out front. Obviously their day wasn't over yet.

Chapter Seven

AUSTIN STOOD IN the kitchen, talking to the police detective who'd arrived along with the uniformed officers when the alarm company hadn't reached anyone at the house. According to the detective, someone had entered through the back door off the kitchen. They'd already done a sweep and the house was clear and safe. Whoever had broken in was gone. They'd shattered the window on the kitchen back door and unlocked it from the inside. The police had had a team come in and check the knob for prints. Everyone agreed the perp had probably worn gloves.

Obviously the alarm had scared them off but had it been before they'd taken anything? He'd done a quick walk through the house. No electronics, televisions, computers, or anything worth money appeared to have been stolen.

He ran a frustrated hand through his hair and glanced at Bailey and Mia from the window over the kitchen sink. Mia had taken her to the swing set to keep her away from the adult talk and chaos inside.

Austin had filled the police in on the custody issue he was having with his ex-wife, although breaking and entering didn't strike him as her MO. She had nothing to gain and everything to lose by taking such an extreme step or persuading someone to help her.

Austin had a call in to his parents and they were on their way to pick up Bailey. He wanted her out of here for the night—or longer. He didn't know what was going on but he didn't like it and he didn't want his daughter at risk.

"You're sure I can let my daughter inside?" he asked the officer who was writing up a report.

"Yes. We checked closets, the basement, and every room in the house. We just have a man going through room by room to see if we missed anything."

Austin opened the window, avoiding the broken glass on the door. "Mia!" he called and waved to her to bring Bailey inside. "Come in through the garage!"

She flashed him a thumbs-up gesture. A few seconds later, they joined him in the kitchen. "Can you take Bailey upstairs to pack? She's going to have a sleepover at her grandparents'." He ruffled his daughter's hair.

Mia nodded in understanding.

"Really??" Bailey asked, obviously surprised.

"They miss you. Let's call it a special occasion," he said to her, forcing an easy smile he didn't feel.

"Okay, Daddy." She unhooked her backpack from her shoulders, where she'd slung it to come inside, and placed it on the kitchen table.

Austin caught sight of an unfamiliar manila envelope on the counter. "What's this?"

"Oh my God." The color drained from Mia's face. "With all the excitement of what happened at school and then the break-in, I completely forgot! Shit." She winced, glancing at Bailey. "I was subpoenaed to testify at a retrial for my old boss."

"I thought he was in jail?" The hair on the back of Austin's neck began to prickle uncomfortably.

"Apparently he got off on a technicality and it took the DA a while to find me since I moved out of state."

"Mia, do you think he has anything to do with the guy who approached you at the supermarket? Or this?" He gestured to the still-broken glass by the back door.

"I… The supermarket definitely. Threats are something he'd do. A break-in?" She shook her head. "He's done nothing like that in my past experience."

"Detective?" A uniformed officer walked out from the hallway where Mia's room was. "I found this on the bed in the extra room down here." He held up a white paper with typing on it.

The detective accepted the sheet. "'Mind your own business,'" he read out loud.

Austin shot Mia a knowing look. "Still so convinced?" he asked her.

"Oh my God. I'm sorry. I mean, I had no idea there even was a retrial until today. I'll pack. I'll go. I would never put you or Bailey in any danger. I'm so sorry." She started for her room but Austin stopped her, grabbing her arm. "Whoa. Slow down. You're not going anywhere."

Panic had rushed through him at her words. She wasn't leaving when she was in trouble. Guarding against it was his specialty and he'd already arranged for Bailey to be away from things for a while. School could wait. She was only six, after all. If she was going to turn to anyone, it would be him.

"But—"

"Please go help Bailey pack. I'll fill the detective in on your situation and you can answer any questions when you're finished. Okay?" He glanced at the other man, not wanting to step on toes.

"Fine. Make it quick," he said to Mia, his gaze softening when he glanced at Bailey.

Austin began to explain Mia's previous employer's trial, conviction, and subsequent release, and while he was doing so, his parents arrived. It took a few minutes to calm his mother down and reassure her the break-in was under control and everyone was safe and would remain so.

Austin's dad stepped up and ushered Bailey and his wife out of the house. Austin kissed his daughter good-bye and promised to video chat with her later. He and Mia finished up with the police, and they said they would let Austin know about anything new they found out.

Finally, the cops were gone, Bailey was safely with his parents, and Mia and Austin were alone.

He walked up to her and grasped both hands in his. "Do you really think I'd let you go through this alone?"

"I think you'd put your daughter first and you should."

"And I did. She's safe with my parents. Now I'm going to take care of you."

She met his gaze, gratitude and something more shining in their depths. "Thank you—"

He pulled her close, cutting her off by sealing his lips over hers. He kissed her hard, wanting her to understand that she was a priority, as much as he didn't want to admit that to himself. He didn't want anything to happen to her and not because being a protector was ingrained in his veins. No, it was because this was Mia and she'd gotten under his skin.

"What am I going to do?" she asked.

"You mean what are we going to do?" he correct-
ed her. "First, I'm going to clean up the mess and
board the window. We'll spend the night here, and
first thing tomorrow, we'll get on the road."

Her eyes opened wide. "Where are we going?"

"The papers say you don't testify for another week
or two. We have time. And I have a cabin upstate.
We're going to get away from everything for a few
days while I think and formulate a plan to deal with
both my ex-wife and your former employer."

"Okay."

"And Mia?"

"Yes?"

His gaze fell on hers. "I plan to pick up where we
left off a month ago. I still want you."

And he meant to have her. They'd have the opportunity to distract each other and forget about their
problems… if only for a little while.

★ ★ ★

Mia had mixed feelings about going away with
Austin. Of course, she was looking forward to being
alone with him, and yes, excited awareness rippled
through her veins, but she couldn't forget the reason
for this trip. It wasn't just about sex; that was the
bonus. This excursion was because someone was
serious about preventing her from testifying. Serious

enough to break into his house, and she felt guilty about bringing trouble to his doorstep and separating him from his daughter.

But after his earlier declaration, *I still want you*, she'd decided to leave her fear behind and savor the time they spent together. She wouldn't overthink things and she definitely wouldn't let herself dwell on the pesky feelings and emotions that could mess up the good thing she had going with him.

There were no heavy expectations and she told herself it worked for her. And it did, as long as she didn't let herself think about all his finer qualities. Like his protectiveness when it came to his daughter and how he'd transferred it to Mia. He could have sent her packing when he realized she was bringing trouble to his doorstep. Instead he'd stepped up and taken charge of her safety. It was hard not to fall for a guy like that… but falling wasn't an option. It wasn't what they'd tacitly agreed to. An affair was all this was, all it could be.

And she intended to enjoy until the real world intruded once again.

She packed and met him out at the SUV parked on the driveway. He wore a pair of jeans and a cream-colored sweater, looking sexy with a pair of aviators covering his eyes.

"Ready?" he asked.

"Yes." She gestured to the carry-on-sized suitcase she'd packed, trying to be practical and not overdo it with too many choices. It wasn't like they were going out to fancy restaurants. They were staying in and she'd chosen accordingly.

He loaded the trunk with their bags and they got on the road. The trip passed in comfortable silence, the discussion mostly about music and other things they liked... and didn't like.

They stopped at a grocery store not far from the cabin and she insisted on food *she* could prepare for them. Cooking relaxed her and she liked taking care of people. He'd gone on about the fireplace he loved at the cabin, and so she added some fun things to the grocery list, hoping he liked her idea later.

Throughout the morning, they were just two people enjoying each other's company. Of course, that was on the surface. Right below was a simmering awareness that she couldn't deny. He'd pushed up the arms of his sweater and her gaze settled on his muscular forearms with a sprinkling of dark hair. Those arms were sexy. The man himself was delicious and she wanted to get her hands on him again. They'd just had that one time together and nothing since except in her daydreams and at night when her subconscious took over and let her imagine him sneaking into her room and taking her hard and fast, slowly and sensually, and many other ways.

He'd made his intentions clear for their time away from the world. And she knew what she wanted, too.

She wanted *him*.

★   ★   ★

AUSTIN LOVED THE cabin. His parents had bought the place as a family getaway and it was his home away from home. He came up here sometimes to get a break from the stress of life. Bailey was too young to join him in the woods or to commune with nature but when his parents took her for the weekend, he'd come here and just... breathe.

He'd never brought a woman to the cabin before. Not before Bailey... and definitely not after. Mia was the first. She was a first in a lot of ways.

The first woman he felt protective over. The first he wanted to spend extended time with. And the first he couldn't get out of his head. He'd tried to convince himself that it was for her safety only that he brought her away from their normal routine. But that didn't explain why last night, when they'd said good night and gone to their own rooms, he'd been hard as nails and had to jerk himself off to thoughts of her before he could get to sleep.

And even then, he'd dreamed of someone coming after her. He planned to make sure he was between

Mia and any shot her ex-employer took at her. It'd just better not be a literal one.

Mia took the spare bedroom in the cabin and he let her. She didn't need to know she'd be sleeping in his bed until she passed out there from sexual exertion.

After a delicious steak dinner, he helped clean up and she shooed him out of the kitchen, claiming she had a surprise.

He threw another log on the fire. It was cooler up-state and the temperatures were low for late October. Being here wasn't the same without the warmth and flickering flames. And this particular day, a fire was romantic.

Another first. Giving a shit about impressing a woman. Especially one he kept telling himself was just a fling until he got her out of his system.

"Ready?" Mia called as she walked out of the kitchen, a tray in her hands.

He rubbed his hands on his jeans and stood. "What's the surprise?" he asked.

"S'mores. When you told me this place had a fire-place, I couldn't resist." She put the tray down on the large ottoman across from the sofa. "Marshmallows, Hershey chocolate bars, and graham crackers. And…"

She picked up a roasting stick in her hand. "Skewers so we can toast the marshmallows." She looked pleased with herself. And with a white sweater falling over and baring one shoulder, she made an extremely irresistible picture.

"Well, then, let's do it."

She clapped her hands together and they each took a marshmallow and put it on a skewer.

"Did you get the chance to do this when you were a kid?" Or had she learned as an adult?

He used to go camping with his dad and he hoped she had some good experiences that indicated normalcy in her childhood.

"I did."

He used the poker to pull open the covering to the flame.

"I had a nice family that taught us to roast marshmallows in a fireplace. Honestly, foster care wasn't all bad."

"I'm glad."

They sat side by side, turning their sticks and roasting their marshmallows.

"So how do you like yours?" she asked. "I prefer them just a little toasty." She pulled hers out earlier than he did and made the s'mores sandwich.

"I like them well done."

"Eew." She bit into her treat and moaned, the sound going straight to his cock. "I love the gooey center." The marshmallow was messy, getting on her cheeks and her lips. Laughing, she licked at her fingers.

He wanted in on that taste. He glanced at his marshmallow, took it out of the flame, and laid it on a plate on the tray she'd brought in.

"C'mere," he said in a gruff voice.

Her laughter died down and she inched her way over to him on her knees. He grabbed her wrist and held it up, straightening her fingers, then sliding the one with the marshmallow goo into his mouth.

He licked, sucked, then grazed her finger, pulling the sticky substance off her skin and into his mouth. "Mmm. I think I want more."

"Go ahead," she said in a husky voice.

He cupped the back of her neck in his hand and pulled her close, gliding his lips over her sticky ones, nibbling on the flesh with his teeth. She gripped his shoulders, her nails digging through his sweater. He devoured her, tasting the combined sweetness of the marshmallow and Mia combined.

Between the heated need swamping her and the warmth from the fireplace, he was beginning to sweat. He broke the kiss. Reaching down, he pulled his sweater off and tossed it aside.

Taking a cue from him, she did the same, leaving her in a sexy bra he had a hunch she'd chosen because they were coming here to be alone. And he appreciated the effort.

He cupped both breasts in his hands and groaned

at the feel of their delicious weight in his hands. He brushed her nipples with his thumbs, toying with the distended peaks until she moaned, arching into his touch.

She slid her fingers to the waistband of his jeans, undoing the button and gliding the zipper down and over the swell of his cock. Any thoughts he had of remaining in control fled at her touch and he let her have her way. Lord knew he'd dreamed of this moment many fucking times over the last few months.

He helped her remove his jeans and kicked them aside, his boxer briefs along with them, leaving his aching cock straining and waiting for her to take charge. She didn't hesitate, wrapping her smaller hand around his shaft.

"Stand up," she said.

He had no problem doing as she instructed. Kneeling, she edged closer, pumped her hand down his cock once, twice, before wrapping her lips over him.

He groaned, sliding his fingers into her hair. He massaged her scalp, promising himself he'd hold on and not fuck her mouth the way he desperately wanted to. This was her show and he intended to let her run it, no matter how much his body demanded otherwise.

She licked over the head, dipping her tongue along the slit and then around the rim. He shuddered and gripped her hair tighter, tugging and silently asking her to move. She picked up a rhythm that had him rocking his hips in time to the laps of her tongue as she pulled him deeper into her mouth.

One hand on his thigh, she moved the other to cup his balls and he nearly came right then. Instead he managed to breathe through the desire to come and let her continue to give him the best damned blow job he'd ever had. Not because of technique but because she put her mind to the task and was wholly focused on him.

Attuned to his moans and thrust of his hips, she kept her licks and the glide, pull, and suck of her lips in time with his need. His body was hers to command and she did, pumping her hand up and down his shaft as his cock glided along her tongue to the back of her throat.

His balls drew up tight, his head swirled, lost to her ministrations and talented tongue. And then she swallowed around him, and it set off an intense climax the likes of which he'd never felt before. She continued to suck and milk him, swallowing all he gave her, not stopping until he'd finished.

She sat back, a satisfied smile on her lips, and he grinned, easing down beside her.

"Looking pretty pleased with yourself."

She laughed. "I got the result I wanted."

"Now it's my turn to get the result *I* want." He

grasped her hips and pulled her toward him, undressing her as quickly as she'd done to him.

Her jeans landed on top of his and he took in her naked body, the sight of her bringing his cock back to life. She amazed him with her ability to arouse him again so quickly.

With her naked body his to play with, he picked her up and carried her in front of the fire, laying her down on the fuzzy rug there. He stretched out beside her, gazing into her eyes, which were hazy with desire and studying him intently.

"I don't know what it is you do to me, but you twist me up inside," he muttered, and before she could reply, he covered her body with his, kissing her hard and fast so she would lose herself in him.

Because he'd sure as fuck lost himself in her.

★   ★   ★

MIA'S HEAD WAS spinning and her body was on fire. Taking Austin in her mouth and making him lose control had been a heady feeling, one that caused her entire being to unravel along with him. Her arousal was at its peak, her sex empty and needy. And when he slid himself on top of her, grinding his ever-hardening erection into her, she nearly came right then.

She gripped his bare ass and arched her hips upward, seeking harder contact, more friction, a faster movement of her sex against his cock. He didn't disappoint her, either. He ground himself into her, pumping his hips until the sensations swamping her became too much.

"Austin!" She cried out his name as she shattered, an orgasm that was spectacular and yet left her pulsing and empty.

He pulled on her hair and she met his gaze. "I'm going to get a condom."

She nodded and barely had time to catch her breath before he was back.

He stood over her, powerful and hard, as he rolled the condom over himself before kneeling down before her.

"Now I'm going to make *you* feel good," he promised, notching himself between her thighs, pushing his cock through her swollen folds, gently at first, then thrusting hard and deep.

She sucked in a shallow breath. The feel of him stretching her was incredible. He'd braced his hands on either side of her head and his gaze was hot on hers as he began to move, sliding himself in and out of her in long, languid strokes.

She wrapped her legs around his lower back, crossing her ankles behind him. The movement joined them even more tightly together and he groaned, his big body shaking with need as he gathered rhythm and began a steady, punishing thrusting that had her seeing stars. The best kind of stars, the ones that glowed and sent her body soaring higher.

She rocked her hips against him as he continued to drive into her, shifting his hips and hitting the right spot inside her. She dug her nails into his back and moaned, a keening, wailing sound she didn't recognize but knew came from her.

"Oh, God."

"No, Austin. Say it," he said, pulling out and pausing.

"Austin!" His name on her lips triggered something primal inside him and he plunged into her over and over again, triggering her orgasm almost immediately. "Oh, God, I feel you."

He groaned and took her harder, her inner walls contracting around him, causing the most exquisite sensations to sweep over her.

His rhythmic thrusts continued until he expelled a harsh breath and came hard, his hips grinding into her over and over until he collapsed, his big body covering hers.

He pulled himself together quickly, rolling to the side because he obviously knew he was crushing her. "Be right back."

He disappeared and returned quickly, kneeling down and scooping her into his arms.

"Where are we going?" she asked, wrapping her arms around his neck.

"To bed so I can rest up and do this all over again." He headed not for the small bedroom she'd chosen for her own but the big master one on the other side of the single-story cabin.

They fell into bed, a tangle of limbs, and passed out, until she woke to the most delicious feeling of his mouth on her sex, licking her awake and into an almost immediate unexpected orgasm. And after she'd come down from that one, he was inside her again, turning her upside down with his skill and attention and essentially ruining her for all other men.

Chapter Eight

M IA WOKE UP first. She rolled over and realized she was sore from the night's activities. She also remembered her last thought before falling asleep for the night... and knew she wasn't wrong. There was something special between her and Austin, something she doubted she'd find again with any other man. He was in tune with her body, her emotions, and attentive to what she needed and when. She was falling for the man and it wasn't hard to do. Not when she was living in his house, taking care of his daughter, and caring about everything he was going through with his ex.

But that was the crux of the problem. His ex-wife had ruined him for future relationships. He'd made that clear to Mia before sleeping with her, so she had no one to blame but herself if he was coming to mean more to her than an easy fling.

She pushed herself out of bed, leaving the sexy man sleeping on his back. The sheet had dipped to his waist, revealing the corded muscles, hot tattoo, and sexy sprinkling of hair trailing down to his waist. He'd flung one arm over his eyes as if covering them from the incoming sun from the window. He breathed in and out in a deep sleep.

She smiled at the sight, turned and headed for the room where she'd put her things, and took a hot shower in the spare bathroom. She changed into a faded pair of jeans and a red and black flannel shirt, tying her damp hair up in a messy bun. Then she walked into the kitchen to make breakfast for them both, determined to put her emotions on lockdown as she'd often done as a child.

Yes, her childhood had been fine, but she'd learned to wrap up her feelings and store them in mental boxes with tight lids that wouldn't, couldn't open up and spill out all the painful things that could hurt her.

Like Christmas, when all the kids at school listed their many gifts and she knew she'd been fortunate to get the one item she received from her foster family. She'd heard stories from the social workers who spoke in hushed voices about the kids who weren't as fortunate, who didn't celebrate Christmas or receive anything for the holiday.

So she'd told herself she didn't care about the number of items, that it was the thought and the one she'd gotten that mattered. Then she'd boxed up the pain she'd felt listening to the others, the hurt that came when she thought about how her parents weren't alive to celebrate with, and pushed it all aside.

And now, as she cracked eggs for their omelets, she boxed up her growing feelings for Austin because he could never, would never reciprocate them, and told herself to be grateful for now. For this weekend in the cabin and her time alone with him. Soon enough they'd have to deal with the problems that awaited them back home.

"Good morning!" Austin strode into the kitchen, freshly showered, his hair damp, wearing a pair of jeans that looked sexy on his muscular frame and a dark grape-colored Henley.

He looked good enough to eat.

"Morning!" she said as she scooped the second omelet she'd made with vegetables, cheese, and eggs onto a plate and placed both dishes on the table.

"Wow. You didn't have to do this." He glanced at the meal. "But I'm glad you did."

She handed him a cup of black coffee the way he liked it and settled into the chair beside him. "My pleasure. So what's on the agenda for today?"

"I thought we'd take a walk. It's beautiful this time of year. And then I figured we'd come back here and fuck like bunnies until the real world intrudes." She caught the sinful look in his eyes as he raised his cup and took a long sip before he turned more serious. "I'm supposed to get a call from the PI I hired. He's due to update me on my ex—and I asked him to pull someone in and get them looking into your former boss. We need to prove he's sending someone after you. Otherwise this shit will keep going on and I won't have it."

Her body went from tingling at the mention of fucking like bunnies... to ice-cold at the reminder of the trouble waiting for her in the real world.

"Most of that sounds like a really good day." She forced a smile.

He covered her hand with his. "Sorry for the blunt reminder. But we're going to get ahead of both things. I have faith."

And she believed in him. "I know." They finished their meal in silence.

A little while later, they pulled on their outerwear and headed for a walk. The air was crisp and it smelled like fall, dry leaves and grass. Her mood lightened at the feel of the cool air on her cheeks and the fresh scents all around her.

To her surprise, Austin reached out and grabbed her hand, holding on as they hiked through the woods. "So... let's just get to know each other," she suggested into the silence. They'd begun on the car ride up but there was more she wanted to know. Little things to learn about him and store away in those mental boxes of hers.

"Okay. Favorite color?" he asked.

"Yellow. Yours?"

"Blue."

She shook her head and laughed. "You're such a typical man. Favorite music?"

"Classic rock," he said.

She eyed him with amusement.

"What?" he asked.

"You're just predictable to me."

They stepped over rocks and crunchy leaves. "Your favorite music?"

She bit down on her lower lip thought she didn't need to think long. "Pop music. Like Taylor Swift and Summer Michelle," she said of the up-and-coming pop star who'd won the television show *Star Power.*

He tugged on her hand and she met his gaze. "Ben, who works for Alpha Security, is engaged to Summer. My bet is you'll be meeting her when her tour comes to New York."

"Oh my God! That's amazing!"

He grinned at her enthusiasm.

"Okay, let's keep going. Favorite drink?" she asked.

"Alcoholic or not?"

She shrugged. "Both."

"Beer... and water. I'm not fussy. You?"

"White Russian and a chai latte."

He laughed. "Okay... favorite holiday?" he asked, picking the next question.

She swallowed hard. "You go first," she said. No matter her sunny outlook on life, holidays had always been hard for her. They always would be.

"Thanksgiving," he said.

"Why?"

"Because it's about family. I like the traditions. You'll see this year." He squeezed her hand more tightly and a little pang hit her in the heart.

Because they'd be his family traditions and she'd be the outsider looking in. Just as she'd always been. The nanny to his daughter, not his girlfriend or someone with meaning to him beyond her paid role. Of course, she was sleeping with him, but that didn't count.

She bit her lip hard to distract herself.

"Mia? I asked your favorite holiday."

"Oh. It's too hard for me to choose," she lied.

She did her best to get through them all. She didn't love any one in particular, because she didn't have wonderful memories associated with them like he did.

He came to a halt, pulling her to a stop when she kept going. She took a few steps back toward him.

"What's wrong? Why are we stopping?"

He smoothed back the hair the breeze had blown onto her cheek and she trembled at his touch. "I'm an insensitive ass."

She blinked up at him, not understanding. "Why would you say that?"

He shook his head. "You go through life so happy. You insist you had such a good childhood that it's easy to believe you and forget… you were in foster care. No matter what you tell the world, it couldn't have been easy. Holidays had to have been hard. And I'm an idiot for not realizing that before I asked that question."

A sudden lump rose to her throat, one she wasn't used to feeling, because like he said, she did go through life happy and mostly grateful. Grateful her life hadn't been worse. That good people had taken care of her. But they hadn't been her parents and nothing could make up for that fact. She just rarely let herself think about it… or remember.

"How did you figure me out?" she asked.

A sad smile lifted his lips. "Oh, I caught your tone of voice. And I know your heart and how hard you try to convince people everything is always great."

"It usually is," she muttered, not wanting to fall apart in front of him. "And that wasn't an insensitive question. And to be honest, I guess it would be

Thanksgiving, too. Because it's the season of giving thanks. I'm grateful for the ability to always look on the bright side."

He tipped her head up with his hand beneath her chin. "You're a special woman, Mia Atwood."

"Thank you." She forced a smile, unnerved by something he'd said, buried in the speech about how well he knew her.

He said he knew her heart.

He couldn't. Or he'd know she was falling in love with him.

★   ★   ★

BACK AT THE cabin, Austin sat in front of the fire. He kicked his feet up on the large ottoman in front of him and stared into the flames.

He couldn't shake his conversation with Mia. How had he never realized how deeply her past affected her? He'd caught the wistfulness in her voice and had immediately realized so much about this warm, loving woman. She gave to everyone without thought to whether or not she'd get back in return.

He ran a hand through his hair, frustrated there was nothing he could do to change what was missing in her life. Nothing but... show her how special holidays could be by sharing his with her. He looked forward to that.

Before he could think further, his cell rang. "Reality intruding," he muttered. A glance at the screen and he was right. "Hey, Dante. What do you have for me?" he asked.

"Your ex is involved with a guy who's heavy into drugs. And considering the guy he met up with last time I tailed him? He's probably into dealing, too."

"You just earned a bonus," he said, beyond pleased. "Tell me you recorded something."

"Photographs. Nothing that'll help you with your ex. Yet. But I'm closer."

Austin blew out a deep breath. "Thank God for small favors. What about info on Parker Alexander?" he asked as Mia walked into the room.

Her eyes opened wide at the mention of her former employer.

He held up a finger, telling her to wait while he gathered details.

"Unfortunately, he lies low. According to my partner, he doesn't meet with anyone, stays holed up in his apartment. I can't get to his phone or computer, so I'm stuck unless he leaves the premises and we can tail him."

Austin shook his head and frowned. "Stay on it," he told the other man.

"Will do. More when I have it." Dante disconnected the call.

"No news?" Mia asked as Austin placed his phone on the leather ottoman beside his opened computer.

"Half and half." He told her what Dante had found out about Kayla's current boyfriend. "So I'm hoping to tie her to drugs and get her out of Bailey's life once and for all. As for your guy... I'm sorry. Nothing yet."

He patted the couch beside him and she eased in next to him. He felt the warmth of her body and his dick growing hard. It didn't take much for him to want her. A look, a glance, a touch.

"Don't worry. We'll find something to prove Alexander is behind the break-in," he assured her.

"I hope so. It's unnerving to think I have to testify with him sitting across from me, knowing he's willing to go pretty far to scare me off."

He pulled her into his arms. "My guys are good—" Before he could go on, the video chat on the computer he had open in front of the sofa interrupted them with a ring.

He shot Mia a regret-filled glance before looking at the name on the screen. Mia scrambled out of his embrace and the screen viewing area, and though he understood why, he felt a pang of regret as he hit accept.

"Bailey Button!" he said as his daughter's little face showed up on the screen. She had high pigtails on either side of her head, obviously courtesy of her grandmother, and she grinned, her missing teeth making him smile. "I miss you!" he said.

"I miss you, too, Daddy." She sounded funny and a deeper look showed him her eyes were glassy.

"What's wrong, princess?" he asked.

"I have a cold." She treated him to a big, deliberate sniff. "And Grandma says I have temperature."

His heart squeezed as it always did when his daughter got sick.

"And I miss Mia," Bailey said on a whine.

He couldn't help but grin. He extended his hand to Mia, out of screen view.

She didn't take it, but she slid closer so she could be in the screen area. "Hey, Bailey. You don't feel well?"

Bailey shook her head. "I miss you," she said again.

"Me, too."

Austin had an easy fix for what ailed her. "How about a visit when I get back?"

She perked up, smiling at his suggestion. "Okay, Daddy. Bring Mia, okay?"

He laughed at the expected request. "Okay."

Bailey took a long sniff and Austin frowned. He hated that she was sick and he wasn't there to take care of her. "Hey. I bet your grandma would give you orange juice if you asked. And I'm also betting grandmas give the best hugs to make you feel better." She smiled, forcing Bailey to grin back.

"Grandma! Can I have orange juice?" Bailey yelled, causing Austin to wince at the decibel level she reached.

"Let me talk to Grandma, kiddo."

Another yell and his mother's face appeared in front of the screen.

"How high is her fever? Did you call Dr. James? I can be home in two hours if she needs me," he said, already thinking about what he needed to do to clean and lock up the cabin. The idea had been in the back of his mind since realizing Bailey was sick.

"Oh my God, Austin. You'd think I didn't raise a child myself!" his mother chided him. "Bailey has a cold. Her ears don't hurt, her throat doesn't hurt, and she's got 100.1. Barely a fever. If it's not gone tomorrow I'll make an appointment. No reason to rush back."

"Okay," he said, relaxing and easing back against the cushions. It was an instinctive reaction to worry.

Just as he worried now about the fact that Mia hadn't taken his hand. He didn't understand and wondered what had happened in the few minutes that had caused her to back off.

"Grandma, orange juice," Bailey said to his mother.

"Please," Austin and Mia automatically said at the same time.

He grinned but she didn't smile in return. He shot her a curious look, wondering what was wrong.

"We'll be home tomorrow anyway. But I need you to keep Bailey for a little while longer. I hope we're close to wrapping up at last one of the problems," he said, not wanting to mention Kayla in front of Bailey and upset her.

"Okay, say bye to Daddy and Mia," his mom said.

"Bye!" Bailey said.

"Feel better," Mia said.

"Love you," Austin added.

No sooner had the screen gone blank than Mia rose and walked across the room. "Is something wrong?" he asked.

She shook her head. "I'm just a little tired. I thought I'd lie down and take a nap."

Considering he'd woken her during the night, her explanation made sense. He believed her... up until she headed for the room with her suitcase and not his bedroom in order to lie down and rest.

MIA STRETCHED OUT on the bed she'd yet to sleep in and stared at the ceiling. She knew she'd overreacted and hadn't made any sense to Austin, not when she'd refused to take his hand or when she'd chosen this room in which to nap. She'd caught the surprised look on his face when she hadn't gone to his bedroom to lie down.

What could she say to him though? That when he'd held out his hand, out of sight from his mother and Bailey, she'd been smacked in the face with the reminder that their relationship was a secret? Would remain a secret? That she wasn't his girlfriend and she shouldn't be spinning ideas about the future just because he'd held her hand when they walked through the woods? Or talked about him sharing the holidays with her and her seeing his family traditions? Or how incredibly intense sex with him just happened to be?

She raised her head, punched the pillow, and turned onto her side. Although she couldn't rationalize all of his actions, like the hand-holding in the woods, she could, however, justify why he'd keep their joined hands out of view of his daughter. Bailey was used to Mia as her nanny. Seeing Mia hold hands with her daddy would only confuse her... and maybe even cause the little girl to spin stories of her own, thinking they were more of a family than was accurate or true.

With the weekened ending soon, it wasn't too soon to start putting her own walls back in place. And if Austin pushed her for answers on her withdrawal... well, the truth would suffice. Because she had no doubt he didn't want a relationship in the true sense of the word. And she was at risk of losing her heart to the man. The same heart that warned her she already had.

Mia didn't realize she'd fallen asleep until she woke up to a knock on her door. She rolled over. The sun had gone down and the room was dark, no light from the windows streaming through.

"Come in!" She pushed herself upright in bed.

Austin opened the door. "Light," he said before he hit the wall switch and the nightstand lamp turned on.

She blinked, her eyes adjusting. He walked into the room, having changed into his favorite relaxing outfit, a pair of black track pants and a random tee shirt. Today's said Alpha on the front... and Security on the back. He always looked sexy, especially now, with wind-tousled hair he hadn't combed and a worried look on his handsome face.

"Sleep well?" he asked, stepping inside.

She nodded. "I guess the fresh air really hit me hard."

He settled on the edge of the mattress, leaning an arm near her hip and taking her hand in his.

His palms were warm as his fingers wrapped around her hand. How did she feel such a simple touch throughout her entire body like she'd touched a live wire?

"I'd like to know what changed," he said, his eyes locking onto hers, not letting her escape his probing gaze and the questions he had. "You froze up during that phone call and rushed to sleep... not in the bed we shared last night."

She sighed, having anticipated his directness. Austin was a straight shooter. "It's just... I was reminded of my place," she said, choosing the simplest explanation.

"Your place." His brow furrowed. "I definitely don't understand." And he still held her hand tightly in his.

She swallowed hard and curled her legs beneath her. She gathered her courage before speaking. "If I'm going to continue to be Bailey's nanny, I can't also be sleeping with you on the one hand and a secret we need to hide from everyone on the other." She couldn't emotionally handle it.

Sex with him had taught her she wasn't equipped for a casual fling. She'd never meant to send him mixed signals, leading him to believe an affair was okay with her when it wasn't. There was no way she could have anticipated the total way he'd taken over her mind, her thoughts, and her heart after she'd gotten involved with him.

"It was amazing, Austin, but we can't have an affair and expect life to go on as normal. We both want different things for our futures. It's best to admit we got it out of our systems and go forward the way we began. As employer and employee."

He stayed silent and she couldn't read him.

"I'm sorry," she said. "I thought I could do casual but apparently it's not in my DNA."

Not that she really knew what was in her DNA. She barely remembered her parents, but sex for the sake of sex apparently wasn't part of her genetic makeup.

He stared at her for a good, long while, and if she didn't know better, she'd think she'd hurt his feelings. But he couldn't be hurt. That would mean their time together meant something special to him and that would leave her thinking he wanted more. Thoughts she couldn't afford to have. Besides, if he was hurt, if he wanted more, he'd tell her and not let her end things.

"I have to respect your wishes," he finally said, letting her hand slip out of his.

She felt the loss, an icy grip taking hold of her heart. "I appreciate that."

He studied her, a frown on his face. "Just so you know… it's not out of my system," he muttered. "*You're* not out of my system."

He wasn't out of hers, either, but it was better to pretend that he was. No way would she admit to him that her biggest fear had been getting attached to him—and she had. And of falling hard for him—and she'd done that, too.

THE NEXT MORNING, the car ride home passed in uncomfortable silence. Austin knew he should behave better but he was pissed. Pissed their weekend had blown up in his face and pissed that he understood why and couldn't change it.

He could promise her exclusivity while they were together but he couldn't offer her a future, and if she couldn't handle that, then she was right. Ending things now was the right thing to do. And he'd fucking have to get over it so he could treat her like his daughter's nanny and not the woman he'd had in his bed. The one he wanted to keep there. But no matter how deeply he cared for her, and he had no doubt that he did, he couldn't bring himself to think beyond a casual affair.

He had a bad history with his ex. Hell, he had a shitty present, and he needed to work on making that issue go away for good. And then he had to focus on raising his daughter. Marriage, family, more kids… were not in his future. And that's what Mia wanted. It's what she deserved after growing up without those ties and being alone for the better part of her life. He couldn't give her that. He was finished with serious commitment other than his child.

It would help if he could bring Bailey home sooner as a buffer between them... and wasn't that a crappy way to think. Bailey was staying at her grandparents' until both threats—her mother and Mia's former employer—were neutralized.

Despite the long trip home, he decided to drop off the bags and head straight to his parents' to see Bailey. Mia agreed with the idea and they made the hour-long trip. True to his mother's prediction, Bailey was already feeling better and bounced around them the entire time they were there, chatting and making them laugh with her crazy stories and antics.

Then it was time to return home and the uncomfortableness between Mia and Austin returned and continued over the next few days.

Mia holed up in her room and Austin spent time in his home office. He busied himself with paperwork for Dan and Alpha Security, conference calls, and scheduling and generally kept busy.

Not that he ever stopped thinking about Mia and the look on her face when she'd ended things, telling him she was reminded of her place. That had hurt him. He'd never want her to feel like an outsider in his life, but unless he let her in, went public with the relationship, called it serious, that's what she was.

Fuck.

He ran a hand through his hair, finding it difficult to get back into his work zone. Thankfully, his cell rang, giving him something else to focus on.

He answered, "Rhodes."

"It's Dante and I finally have something solid." He went on to detail information that was going to guarantee Austin custody of Bailey.

It was the first good news of the day and he intended to make use of it. He headed to the kitchen and poured himself a glass of scotch, taking a long sip, the burn feeling as good as the sense of relief filling him at the thought of keeping his child and banishing her unworthy mother from her life for good.

"Hey. Are you okay? Drinking during the day isn't like you," Mia said, joining him and leaning a hip against the counter.

His gaze dropped to the dip of her sweater, the swell of her breasts, and he swallowed a groan. His one-track mind when it came to remembering how her sweet pussy felt around his cock wasn't going to help him treat her like an employee. Hell, she didn't just work for him, she was a friend. More than that, but right now she was someone he wanted to confide in.

"I got good news, so consider this like a celebration." He raised his glass.

"Care to share?" she asked. "The information, not

the drink," she said, laughing.

The light, happy sound twisted his stomach in knots.

"I absolutely do." He took another sip and placed the glass onto the counter, meeting her gaze. "Kayla's boyfriend is dealing drugs from her apartment. Dante has proof. And we have a strategy that will guarantee me my daughter and get Kayla out of my life for good."

Mia's eyes lit up at his words.

She, of all people, understood the importance of his news. She knew how much Bailey meant to him, how much Kayla's threats were eating away at him. The fear of losing the one person in his life who meant the world to him, who defined him, who he'd do anything for had petrified him even if he'd done his best not to show it.

"Kayla can be darn persuasive when she sets her mind to convincing someone about her point of view," he said.

He shook his head at the memories of her telling him she was pregnant, explaining through tears how much she wanted a family and how she loved him. He'd bought her act.

"I don't want her anywhere near a judge. And now she won't be."

Mia clapped her hands and squealed with glee.

"What's your plan?"

"I'm going to call her and ask to meet. Explain I have some terms I'd like to discuss with her. Let her think I'm coming around to her way of thinking, that maybe she'll see a payday. At which point I'll lay out my evidence, tell her that, as we speak, the police are searching her apartment and arresting her boyfriend. And just happen to be outside the restaurant waiting to bring her in for questioning. She won't see Bailey again. Ever," he said on a low growl.

"Oh, Austin." Without hesitation, she stepped forward, wrapped her arms around his waist, and held him close. "I'm so relieved for you."

Despite everything that had passed between them, despite her having pulled back, she was here for him now. He ran a hand down her silky hair. He bent his head and inhaled her fragrant scent, the hint of citrus and freshness he always associated with her causing his dick to harden as want filled him.

"Mia," he groaned.

She tipped her head up, meeting his gaze, her lips offered up to him—even if that wasn't her intent.

Intent or not, he needed a taste. One last taste if that's what it turned out to be. He captured her lips with his, gliding his tongue over the seam, waiting for the breathy moan sure to follow, and when she gave it up, he slid deeper inside. He kissed her hard, grasping her face and turning her first one way, then another, anything to devour all of her.

She rose onto tiptoes, pressed her body into his, her breasts smashed against his chest, her arms coming to wrap around his neck, her fingers curling up and into his hair. His hands dropped to her waist and he pulled her into him, his cock rubbing sensually against her stomach. He throbbed painfully and it must have been his thick erection that sunk into her consciousness, because she jerked back, stepping out of his arms.

"No. I don't want to send mixed signals," she said, dismay and unhappiness etched on her face as she spoke through her puffy, well-kissed lips. "And we shouldn't do that again... I just wanted to let you know how happy I am for you about Bailey. I didn't mean—"

"I know," he assured her. "*I* did it. Because I can't resist you. But I will try harder. And you can consider this helping me celebrate. Nothing more."

Except it was. Kissing her was everything.

Chapter Nine

M IA DECIDED TO beat Austin to the kitchen early the next morning. She wanted to fuel him with coffee before his meeting with his ex-wife. She'd set her alarm knowing what time he usually came downstairs, but she hadn't planned to find it so difficult to get out of bed. No sooner had she sat up than nausea swamped her and she lay back down until the wave passed, staring at the ceiling and praying to feel better.

She tried to sit up again, this time with more positive results. Nothing more fun than a stomach bug, she thought wryly, but she pushed on and managed to shower, feeling semi-okay once she'd dressed.

Her cell phone rang just as she was ready to go to the kitchen. She didn't recognize the number but it had a New York area code. Her stomach churning even more now, she answered the call.

"Hello?"

"Mia? It's Kate Collins, the Manhattan district attorney. I assume you received the summons to appear?"

"Oh, hi, yes. I did. I'm surprised you didn't call me first."

"I'm sorry about that. I was in court on a case and we had to get this moving. I'd like you to come to the city for some trial prep."

Mia swallowed hard. "Sure. Whatever you need."

"Great. I'll be in touch with the day and time."

"Thank you," Mia said, and Kate uttered good-bye and disconnected the call.

Mia pinched the bridge of her nose and breathed in deep, holding back the nausea that wasn't courtesy of the phone call.

She headed out to the kitchen and made herself a cup of tea, which worked to settle her queasy stomach, at least until she brewed coffee for Austin. She breathed in, smelled the aroma, and ran for the bathroom. She threw up the tea and not much else since her stomach was empty.

She brushed her teeth and washed her face, glancing in the mirror over the towel as she dried off. Ugh. Her face was pale, her eyes glassy. But she felt better again after losing what little was in her stomach, and she walked out to talk to Austin before he left.

She found he'd already poured himself a cup of coffee when she arrived, and this time, her stomach didn't clench at the smell. "Good morning."

"Morning." He lifted the cup to his sexy mouth and took a sip. "You're pale," he said, meeting her gaze. "Are you okay?"

She blushed at the mess she looked like, but when you lived in the same house as someone, there wasn't much you could do to disguise the bad days. "Yeah. I... um... I wasn't feeling well earlier but I think I'm better now."

He glanced at her with concern in his eyes. "Well, rest today. It's not like Bailey is around to keep you hopping, so take advantage."

She smiled. "I will." She hesitated, wondering if she should apologize again for what had happened between them yesterday.

She had to learn to live in the same house with him even when Bailey wasn't around. She couldn't kiss him one minute and push him away the next, sending mixed signals because her body and heart wanted what her mind knew she couldn't have.

She sighed and pushed that thought away. There were more pressing concerns going through her mind.

"Austin," she said, knowing she had to tell him about her phone call. "The district attorney called me this morning. She wants me to come into the city for trial prep. I realize Bailey's not home, so it shouldn't be an issue, but I thought you should know."

"Shit. I wish you didn't have to deal with this again."

She nodded. "Me, too. But I'll just take the train—"

"No. I told you I'll make sure you're safe while you deal with this and I will."

"Thank you. I'm truly grateful. I just… It's not fair to you. Any of this. I know you want to bring Bailey home as soon as possible, especially once this situation with her mother is resolved, and thanks to me, you can't." She ran her hands up and down her arms over her sweatshirt, rubbing away the sudden chill.

His eyes warmed at the mention of his daughter and immediately squinted in displeasure at her follow-up conclusion. "Of course I want to bring her home but this is not your fault. Things happen. We deal with them."

"We do, but this is my problem, not yours. And I don't want to keep messing up your life. So I…" She swallowed past the words but they had to come out. "I could move out," she offered, sick at the thought. But she'd do it for Austin's sake. For Bailey's.

"What?" he asked, obviously shocked.

She held up a hand, wanting him to listen before he decided. "It makes sense. Think about it. You could have your daughter home and not have to worry about my problems with my former employer. I'll come back after his trial is over, or after I testify… that is, if you still want me." She rushed out her thoughts, knowing it was what was best for Bailey. For Austin.

"No."

She blinked at his abrupt tone. "But—"

"No buts." He placed his mug down and strode over so he was looming over her, big and powerful and sexy. "First, I'm a bodyguard. A protector by nature. Do you really think I would send you out there knowing someone was willing to break into this house to send you a message?"

"I guess not," she murmured, not the least bit taken aback by his harsh voice. She understood where his anger was directed and it wasn't at her.

"That's right. I'm going to protect you up until and through your testimony."

Appreciation along with a shiver of awareness trickled through her at his determined tone and proclamation. "Thank you."

He inclined his head, his darkened gaze boring into hers. "I'm not going to let anyone harm you."

She believed him.

He reached for her, then obviously thought better of it and shoved one hand into his pocket. With the other, he reached for his coffee mug and took a final sip of his coffee.

It hurt, she thought, his pulling back, but reminded herself she had made the decision first. Not him. She was the one who couldn't handle casual and not get her heart hurt. So if he was following her lead, who was she to argue?

"Along those lines, while I'm gone, I have someone outside watching the house. After the break-in, I didn't want you home alone."

She nodded. "Thank you. I'm grateful." And overwhelmed by the lengths he'd go to in order to keep her safe.

"I should get going," he said, glancing away. "I don't want to be late for this meeting with Kayla. The sooner I get her out of our lives for good, the better."

Mia nodded. "Can I get you a travel mug to take with you?" she offered.

"That would be great. I could use some more caffeinated fortification."

She pulled a mug from the cabinet and drew a deep breath as she poured the coffee, doing her best not to over-inhale and upset her stomach again. She felt better, but in a fragile, it's-still-there sort of way.

She closed the mug with the cover and handed it to him, careful to avoid their fingers touching.

"Thank you. Listen, I need to ask you something," he said. "I have to go to a party this weekend at my boss's house."

"That's nice," she murmured.

"And I don't want you home alone. Not after

someone broke in with the alarm set. Plus, the party is to celebrate Summer Michelle and my pal Ben's return to the States after a short European tour and I know how much you'd love to meet her. Being that she's your favorite pop star." He winked at the reminder of their walk in the woods and the get-to-know-you questions that they'd indulged in.

She remembered in detail… how small her hand felt in his, how warm and sensual his skin was wrapped around her palm. Just like how hot and strong his naked body felt when it came down over hers. She trembled and shook her head in an attempt to dislodge the thoughts that had no place in her mind right now.

"The point is," he went on, oblivious to the turn her mind had taken, "I want you to come with me to Dan's."

"Dan?" she asked stupidly, still lost in being with Austin in all the ways she'd pushed away.

He wrinkled his brows, obviously confused. "Dan, my boss. You've heard his name before."

"Yes. Of course. Sorry. I'm still a little queasy," she said, blaming her stomach for her frazzled behavior.

This time he did reach out and lift her chin with his hand. "Are you okay?" he asked, seriously worried as he looked into her eyes.

She did her best not to get lost in his. "Yes. I think

I might have picked up a stomach virus or something. I'll rest today. And as for your party… I'll go with you," she said.

She wished she was going as his date but again it all came down to choices. And what she could and couldn't live with. Besides, who knew, even if they were together, if he'd have taken her as anything more than a means to keep her safe. Or to allow her to meet her favorite pop star.

★ ★ ★

AUSTIN DRANK FROM the travel mug Mia had made him, trying his best to focus on the road, but he had so much on his mind, not the least of which was his ex, who he was meeting with, hopefully for the final time, and Mia, who he'd left home not feeling well and dealing with trial shit that should have been in her past.

He was so used to her being perky and happy that seeing her sick had thrown him. With her pale coloring and glassy, big green eyes, he'd wanted to pick her up and carry her to bed. He'd wanted to take care of her in the most primal, elemental way.

Which made no sense to him. He took care of his daughter. Women were secondary. Or had been until Mia.

He gripped the steering wheel harder and forced

himself to concentrate on how he planned to handle Kayla, which meant he was prepared when he walked into the diner and caught sight of her sitting alone at a table, drinking a cup of coffee like she didn't have anything to worry about except collecting her paycheck.

He strode over and settled into a seat, facing his duplicitous, smug-looking ex-wife, who sat drumming her fingertips on the table. She wore a satisfied smile on her face and a tight dress, though she had to know he was immune to anything she had or tried to offer.

"I'm so glad you called," she practically purred. "I knew you'd come around to my way of thinking."

He forced a smile. "I decided it was time we talk terms."

He could see the dollar signs in her eyes and the pleasure he was about to get magnified tenfold.

"So." She trailed her fingers across the table until she curled her hand around his. "What are you willing to give me?"

He jerked his hand away. There were things he would not allow her to do and touching him was high on the list. "You know, I should be grateful to you, Kayla. Sounds crazy, I know, but poking holes in that condom gave me my greatest gift."

He thought of the little girl who looked more like him than her mother, with her toothless grin and happy laugh, and everything inside him eased.

Kayla nodded, a satisfied grin forming on her heavily colored lips. "I'm glad you can see the upside in this situation. I have to say I'm surprised you're being so generous with the compliments."

Yes, he thought, he was buttering her up and setting her up for the fall. And damned if he wasn't enjoying every minute. "So you see, there really isn't much I wouldn't do in order to keep my daughter with me and… safe from you."

She frowned at that. "I'm hardly a monster."

"I suppose we can agree to disagree on that."

"Excuse me," a waitress said, coming up to the table with a pot of coffee in hand. "Can I get you something to drink before you order?" she asked. "A refill?" She glanced at Kayla, who had arrived first.

"No thank you," he told her. "Actually I won't be ordering."

"I'll take a refill," Kayla said, completely at ease with whatever was coming next.

Just the way he wanted her.

The waitress topped off her cup and Kayla added her milk and Splenda, and Austin gave her all the time she needed. "So where were we?" she finally asked.

"Disagreeing on how to describe your personality, but that's neither here nor there."

"I agree. Last time you gave me a hundred grand.

This time—"

"You're not getting a penny."

She slammed her hand down, rattling the table and splattering her coffee over the top of the cup. "How do you figure? Because I know you don't want to end up in front of a judge."

He smiled, his first genuine one since sitting down across from her. "Actually that's exactly what I want. Because like I told you, there is very little I won't do to protect my daughter. Starting with hiring a private investigator to look into your life, and it's very interesting what he discovered."

Kayla stared at him in disbelief. "I doubt there's anything that could prevent me from getting custody." But a tic had formed at the corner of her eye and she attempted to cover up her nerves with a shake of her dark hair over her shoulders.

He rested his arms on the table. "Think again. I've got photographs of your live-in boyfriend, Paul Milian, dealing drugs from your apartment. Video, too. Oh, and guess who happened to be standing right there when the transaction took place?"

Her mouth opened wide before she pursed her lips in feigned annoyance. "I know nothing about that. Paul's business is of no concern to me. You know I can get any judge to—"

"To throw your custody suit out when he finds out

you're living with a drug dealer," Austin said. "Nice area you're living in, by the way. I guess you're that hard up for cash. Or maybe you have a habit of your own you need to support and that's why you're trying to blackmail me for money? Either way, you're finished."

Kayla's eyes narrowed and he could see the calculations going on in her brain. "Oh, you know better than that. I don't give up that easily." But her hands were shaking and he hadn't even told her the best part.

"As we speak, the police are searching your apartment with a valid warrant. If your boyfriend is there, I can guarantee you he's been arrested."

Now real fear replaced the smug look of earlier. "I need to go."

Austin glanced over and nodded at the men seated at a nearby table. Then he leaned back in his seat and let them do their jobs.

They rose from their chairs and walked over. "Kayla Gibson?" the taller man asked, pulling out a badge from his jacket pocket.

His ex swallowed hard. "Yes."

"I'm Officer Suarez and this is my partner, Officer Harrison. We'll need you to come downtown for questioning." The officers had given Austin the professional courtesy of wrapping up his blackmail issue with his ex-wife before stepping in.

The color drained from her face. "Whatever you want, it has to be a mistake."

"We can assure you it's not," Officer Suarez said. "Drugs were found in your apartment this morning. Now you can come with us quietly or we can make this harder." He parted his jacket, revealing handcuffs he'd obviously be more than happy to use.

With any luck, an arrest was imminent based on the findings in her apartment.

"Good-bye, Kayla. I can guarantee you no judge is going to find you to be a qualified parent now."

"I hate you," she spat at him.

"The feeling is mutual. Now go along with the officers like a good girl." He waved good-bye and leaned back in his seat, satisfaction along with a deep sadness filling him.

Because no matter what, at the end of the day, Kayla was his daughter's mother and that was a sad thing for his little girl. But he intended to make damned sure she had a wonderful life and lacked for nothing. He just couldn't make up for her not having a mom.

He drove directly home, anticipating sharing the news with Mia that the custody issue was over. Nobody would share his excitement like she would. But when he let himself into the house, it was too quiet. The door to her room was open and she wasn't in there, so he headed for the kitchen and family room.

"Mia?" he called out.

"In here."

He walked toward the sound of her voice and found her on the couch.

"Hey." He leaned down beside her, clasping her clammy hand in his. "What's wrong?"

"I came into the kitchen to make something to eat and I got so nauseous. I had to lie down. I guess I fell asleep." She tried to push herself to a sitting position but he held her back.

"Don't. I'm going to take you to bed. Then, if you're hungry, I'll make you something to eat."

Her eyelids fluttered. It was obviously a struggle for her to keep them open. "I don't want to be a burden."

This woman, he thought with a shake of his head. As if she could ever be a problem.

"Shh." He brushed her hair off her face before picking her up and lifting her into his arms. He headed through the kitchen, but instead of going toward her room, he turned to go up the stairs.

"Where are we going?" she asked drowsily.

"Somewhere you can rest… and I can keep an eye on you."

His room, to be exact, but he didn't want to give her something to argue about by telling her. And since her eyes were already closed, he didn't think she'd object right now.

★   ★   ★

MIA WOKE UP slowly. Her head hurt because her stomach was empty but she didn't think she was nauseous anymore. But she was warm. Very warm and she became aware of the hard, hot male body aligned with hers.

Austin.

Her heart began beating too fast in her chest as she realized he lay up against her, his body wrapped around hers, his arm draped around her waist, pulling her close. Her body thrummed with awareness.

She opened her eyes, looked around, and realized this wasn't her room. It was his. She swallowed hard. She remembered feeling sick after a trip to the kitchen and lying down on the sofa. Then he came home, found her, and carried her to her bed.

The sweet man. The sweet, sexy, protective man. He was going to kill her with his kindness and caring while she was supposed to be guarding her heart against his potent appeal.

She wondered if she could roll out from beneath his weight and slip away without waking him. No sooner had she shifted than he groaned, the sound reverberating through her.

"What time is it?" he asked, not letting go of her.

She blinked and glanced at the clock on his nightstand. "Four," she said. She'd slept the day away. "Umm … why am I in your bed? With your arm around me?"

Instead of releasing her, he hugged her tighter. "You're in my bed because I wanted to be able to keep an eye on you if you needed anything. And as for the other, I fell asleep and it just happened."

She noticed he didn't apologize for it, either. "Thank you." But this was not a position she needed to be in and she pushed herself to a sitting position, forcing him to release his hold.

He stretched and sat up beside her, running a hand over his messed hair, which, damn him, gave him a hot, just-had-sex kind of appearance. While no doubt she looked like death warmed over.

"How are you feeling?" he asked, his tone worried.

She took a minute to catalogue how she felt now that she was upright. A little underlying queasiness. Damn. She'd hoped she really was all better.

"Not perfect but better," she admitted. "But I should go."

"No, you should let me get you food. You passed out before eating. Did you have anything earlier?" he asked, giving her a knowing glance.

"No." She bit down on her lower lip. "But I can

take care of it myself."

He shook his head. "That would be a no. I don't want to worry about you fainting or getting nauseous again, so sit tight and I'll be back with toast." He rolled out of bed.

She was grateful to see he was still dressed and she wore her sweats and a tee shirt. She still desired him too much, wanted him too badly to have any kind of temptation adding to this situation.

He headed downstairs and she tossed herself back against the pillows. "What are you doing?" she asked herself.

She was letting him take care of her... and enjoying knowing that he cared. She was torturing herself with what she couldn't have. While he was gone, she went into his bathroom, a nice-sized room with a Jacuzzi tub, a shower with extra spray jets, and a neutral-colored décor. It suited him.

She took care of business and washed her face, brushing her teeth with toothpaste and her finger before rinsing. She felt cleaner, at least, and marginally better. Heading back to bed, she settled in to wait.

He returned a short time later with toast and jelly along with a cup of tea, placing both on the nightstand.

"Thank you." She picked up the cup and took a sip, finding the tea sugared, just the way she liked it.

Her heart warmed at the fact that he noticed. Why was he such a contradiction? A man who didn't want commitment on one hand, taking such good care of her and even noticing things no one else in her life had ever paid attention to before?

"So how did things go with Kayla?" she asked, refusing to dwell on what she couldn't change.

"It went just as I intended. She won't be an issue for me or Bailey anymore." But despite the good news, his smile held a hint of sadness as did his tone.

"What's wrong?"

"I'll tell you if you eat." He gestured to the toast on the nightstand.

She couldn't help but smile at his insistence. "Fine." She picked up a piece of toast and took a bite. The sweetness from the jelly satisfied a craving she hadn't known she had. But Austin clearly had.

"Well?" She tipped her head, indicating it was his turn to talk.

He breathed out a long breath. "When all was said and done, I was thrilled I got what I wanted and Kayla won't be trying to take my daughter from me anymore."

"But?" Because something was obviously on his mind.

His lips lifted at her obviously correct conclusion. "But I couldn't help but feel bad when the cops took her away. I don't like her but this is my kid's mother. I'll have to explain things to Bailey when she's older and it's going to hurt her."

Mia placed the toast back on the plate. "Hey. You tried your best to make the marriage work. You didn't tell her not to be a caring parent." She didn't use the word abusive, although that's what her actions had been. "You only pushed when you had no other choice to protect your daughter." She wanted him to see the facts and not feel guilty that he'd acted against Bailey's mom.

"You're right." He ran a hand through his hair. "It doesn't make me feel any better, but thank you. I did need the reminder."

"Because you're a good man."

His lips curled in a warm smile. Then he tipped his head again. "Now keep eating."

She rolled her eyes, picked up the toast, and finished both pieces, feeling much better once she followed that up with the warm tea.

Chapter Ten

THE DAY OF the party at Austin's boss's house dawned bright and chilly. Mia was still queasy but she was living with it, knowing that eventually the virus would pass. Except it had been almost five days and she was starting to get nervous. Stomach viruses typically lasted a short time. Food poisoning wasn't possible. So there wasn't much of a reason for the nausea to persist except for the one she didn't want to think about.

So she didn't. Not yet. She would still hope for possibility that this was temporary and not life altering.

If she looked ahead, thank goodness things were getting closer to wrapping up with her ex-boss. On Wednesday she would to go to the city and go through trial preparation against Parker, and the thought didn't help her stomach issues, that was for certain.

She had no problem telling what she'd seen, what she'd taped, or what she'd heard and reported to the police. She just dreaded the cross-examination. It was brutal and ugly and she hated the whole process. But she knew the district attorney would go over the usual suggestions: give short answers, only answer what they ask, don't go off on tangents, and tell the truth. Right. While Parker glared daggers at her across the room.

She placed a hand over her stomach and breathed in deep. It was time to get dressed. When asked, Austin had insisted she should be casual for Dan's party, but Mia was meeting Summer Michelle, a woman she'd admired from afar since her days on *Star Power*. Her voice, her talent, and how she'd risen above a viral video that could have derailed her career but somehow only made it stronger, all were things to respect. Plus, she was famous. It was a cool thing and Mia wanted to look good.

Not to mention she was meeting Austin's friends and coworkers and she hoped to make a decent impression. So she chose a pair of jeans in deference to dressing casual, and her favorite cold-shoulder shirt and a pair of black boots. She pulled her hair into a deliberately messy bun and added makeup to cover her pale cheeks. And then she headed to meet up with Austin in the kitchen.

AUSTIN PULLED UP to Dan's, a white house with black

shutters, and from the cars along the street, they weren't the first ones there. Mia had been quiet on the way and he was worried she still didn't feel well. But she didn't seem to want to talk and he gave her space until they pulled up to the curb and he parked.

"You ready to go in?" he asked.

"Yep." She flashed him an obviously forced smile.

"Hey." He placed a hand over hers. "Are you sure you're okay?"

She nodded. "I am. And I'm excited to meet Summer… and of course your friends. So let's go!"

He shot her a concerned look, not really buying the *I'm fine* claim, but what could he do?

He led her to the house, and before they could open the door, it flung open. "Austin!" Dan said. "I saw you coming up the walk and I wanted to greet you and your pretty guest."

Austin glanced at Mia, who blushed at the compliment. "Dan, this is Mia Atwood. Mia, meet Dan Wilson, my boss."

"A pleasure," Mia said with a smile. "Thank you for having me over."

"The pleasure is mine. Come in, you two. Everyone is in the kitchen. You know how it is," he said to Austin. "We all gravitate there." He laughed and gestured inside the house.

Austin led Mia toward the kitchen and family

room, where his friends and coworkers had congregated.

He introduced Mia to Ava Talbott, Jared Wilson, Dan's son, and Ben Hollander. The other members of the team, Shane Landon and Tate Shaw, were away doing freelance work, which made it a small party.

"Where's Summer?" Austin asked, knowing how much Mia wanted to meet the pop star and Ben's fiancée.

"I'm here!" Summer strode out from the back of the house, a wide smile on her face.

With her jet-black hair and stunning, wide brown eyes, she was beautiful. These days Austin preferred petite blondes with green eyes, but he could appreciate Ben's good fortune.

"It's good to see you!" Austin pulled her into a friendly hug.

"You, too."

Ben wrapped an arm around her shoulders.

"Summer, this is my—Mia Atwood." Austin wasn't sure what he'd been about to say and he quickly changed the subject. "Mia's a huge fan."

Summer flushed. "I still can't get used to people saying that," she murmured.

"It's well deserved," Mia said. "I'm so glad to meet you. I love your music."

"Thank you."

"Hey, man, let's let the women talk. I want to catch up," Ben said. "I hear Dan has some fun new gadgets in his office. Let's go check things out in there."

Austin shot Mia a questioning glance and she nodded, a big smile on her face. Obviously she was feeling better because she definitely didn't mind being left with Summer.

He gave her shoulder a squeeze, a gesture that he needed more than her, if only to reassure himself she was fine. Her mood lately had been off, at least since she'd been sick.

He and Ben each grabbed a bottle of beer before Austin followed Ben out of the kitchen and down the hall, past the bathroom to Dan's office. He'd broken down a wall, making two rooms into one large room so that when he worked from home, he could still monitor things going on with work.

Austin rolled the bottle between his hands, not really in the mood for a drink.

"It is good to be home," Ben muttered, sinking into a chair across from Dan's big oak desk.

"I bet. Where are you staying?" Ben and Summer both had apartments in the city.

"My place is bigger, so we moved in there." Ben tipped back the bottle for a sip. "But I want to find something larger. More space, more … I don't know.

Windows." Ben laughed.

"So what's it been like?" Austin asked his friend. "Insane fans and living out of hotels?"

"Pretty much but I have to tell you, as long as I'm with Summer, it's all good." Ben's satisfied smile said it all. He was settled and happy with his choices.

"I'm happy for you. Where are Dan's new gadgets?" Austin asked, glancing around the room and seeing only the usual monitors, cabinets, and documents scattered around.

Ben grinned. "Actually I just wanted to catch up and didn't know how much you'd talk around your guest."

He eyed Austin carefully but he didn't flinch, unwilling to give up information to his suddenly nosey friend.

Ben rolled his shoulders and let out a heavy sigh. "Fine. Let's get specific. Dan tells me you had some issues with the ex? You wrap that up okay?"

"I did. Thank fucking God." Austin blew out a calm, relieved breath.

The kind he'd been exhaling since taking care of Kayla and receiving a call from the cops that they'd booked her along with her boyfriend for selling and possession.

Ben nodded his approval. "And how is your cute kid?"

"Good." At the mention of Bailey, Austin grinned. "But she'll be better when I can bring her home." He explained Mia's current situation to his friend. "I just want that wrapped up before I take Bailey from my parents. Just to be safe. But I've been visiting often."

"I get that." Ben tipped the bottle, taking a sip of his beer. "So what about you?"

"What about me?" he asked warily. What else had they been talking about if not Austin's life? What else was there?

"So last time someone brought a strange woman to one of Dan's parties—"

"You were protecting her?" Austin filled in the end of the sentence before Ben could leap to another conclusion.

He snorted. "I was going to say, I wanted her. And I'm wondering what's going on with you and Mia."

Austin blew out a long breath. He placed the bottle down on a table and met Ben's gaze. Obviously his friend wasn't going to let him off the hook and it wasn't like he couldn't use a friend to talk to. "If I was going to get serious about anyone, it would be Mia. But—" How did he explain?

"You're still fighting the inevitable. I remember those days well. I got it." Ben shook his head in definite understanding and commiseration.

It wasn't the same thing. Ben's history and issues

had been with Summer herself. Austin's problems were tangled up with betrayal and hurt and a little girl he couldn't afford to put in the middle of something and have her get hurt.

"I can't let myself get serious again. I can't risk Bailey getting attached and me deciding it's not working out."

Ben rolled his eyes. "You're certainly very protective of Mia, considering you brought her here when you could have just had someone watch the house."

Austin frowned at his friend.

"I'm telling you, all the fighting you are doing with yourself? It's not worth it. You could have a real family, you know?"

He swallowed hard. He knew. And that was what scared him. Having it. Trusting it. Relying on it. And having the rug ripped out from under him once more. "I've done the family thing once, Ben. Not doing it again."

Except Mia wasn't Kayla, a voice in his head told him. And his friend's knowing shake of his head let Austin know he was thinking the same thing.

MIA LISTENED TO Summer talk about her tour, the adjustments to living on the road, out of hotel rooms, the fans, the venues… all things she wanted to hear about but none she could concentrate on because the nausea had returned. And out of the blue, Mia knew. This couldn't possibly be a stomach virus. She knew better. She wouldn't suddenly want to throw up after five days if it was.

Could she really be pregnant?

Dread and fear took hold as the possibility took root. And grew. She hadn't wanted to believe it, think it, or face it. Hadn't wanted to consider what it would mean for the life she lived. And loved. Or her future.

Or what Austin would think.

Austin, who'd been in this position once before, having gotten a woman pregnant. True, Mia hadn't poked holes in the condom but he hadn't originally wanted or planned that child. And he had no desire to get serious again.

Oh my God, she thought, as another wave of queasiness hit her.

Unaware, Summer continued, a smile on her face. "And Ben said if it wasn't the last stop, he'd pull the plug on the tour because he couldn't wait to get home," Summer said, her voice trailing off as she met Mia's gaze. "Are you okay?" she asked.

"Umm…" She touched Summer's arm. "I don't mean to be rude but I'll be right back."

"Okay."

Before Summer could even get the word out, she

turned and found Dan. "Where's the bathroom?" she asked him, embarrassed but having no choice. She couldn't wait.

"Through there." He gestured toward the main part of the house, where the bedrooms must be. "Down the hall, first door on the left."

"Thank you." She walked very quickly in the direction he pointed and found the bathroom door closed. She heard someone moving around inside, so she leaned against the wall to wait.

She breathed in deeply, counting in and out, forcing herself to concentrate on anything other than throwing up or the very real possibility that she might be pregnant. Or what she would do if she was.

. Suddenly the sound of male voices reached her from the room right next to where she stood. She glanced in that direction. The door was open but she couldn't see inside, but she recognized the voices.

"And I'm wondering what's going on with you and Mia," Ben asked.

A pause and then, *"If I was going to get serious about anyone, it would be Mia. But…"* Austin trailed off.

Mia's stomach cramped, which was not good for her current situation. As wrong as it was, she stood rooted to the spot, listening.

"You're still fighting the inevitable. I remember those days well. I got it," Ben said.

Mia held her breath.

"I can't let myself get serious again. I can't risk Bailey getting attached and me deciding it's not working out."

"You're certainly very protective of Mia, considering you brought her here when you could have just had someone watch the house." Another pause and then Ben went on. *"I'm telling you, all the fighting you are doing with yourself? It's not worth it. You could have a real family, you know?"*

"I've done the family thing once, Ben. Not doing it again."

Now her stomach lurched and luckily the bathroom door opened. Ava Talbott walked out. "Hi, Mia."

"Hi. Excuse me." She made a beeline around the other woman and ran into the bathroom, closing the door behind her.

Long after she'd thrown up and cleaned up, she remained in the bathroom... heart pounding, head throbbing, and heart hurting at Austin's words.

I've done the family thing once, Ben. Not doing it again.

Clearly she had a lot of thinking to do. Of course, she had to be certain before she could make decisions. And to do that, she needed a pregnancy test. Austin hadn't let her out of his sight but she did have an idea to get one.

She calmed down, patted her cheeks for color, and walked out of the bathroom.

They didn't stay at the party long. Austin took one

look at her and knew she had gotten sick again. He was obviously used to her just-vomited look.

Once they were in the car, she turned his way. "I'm really sorry. I could have stayed."

He shook his head. "I'd rather you rest. You have a busy week coming up."

She nodded. "Can I ask a favor? Can we stop by a drugstore on the way home?" She placed her hand over her purse in her lap.

"Sure. I'll run in for you."

She shook her head, having anticipated this gesture. "It's okay. It's, umm… that time of the month and I need a few things."

"Got it," he said with a grin.

Half an hour later, she ran into the drugstore by herself, took care of the things she needed, and returned to the car.

"Got everything?" he asked when she let herself back inside.

"Yes. Thank you," she said, shaking the plastic bag full of sanitary napkins and tampons she more than likely didn't need.

Unless the two pregnancy tests tucked safely in her purse showed she was panicking for no good reason.

Mia decided to take the tests separately. She didn't

know why or what good it would do but she'd convinced herself two separate urine streams would yield the right results. It didn't matter that she was being completely irrational. The fact was, she'd slept with Austin the first time over a month ago, and though they'd used protection, it did have a fail rate. She could very well be pregnant.

She watched the first stick, waiting endlessly... then finally turned away. A watched pot and all that. She paced the bathroom, which was all of a few steps in one direction, another few in the other, rubbing her arms with her hands. This time her stomach churning had everything to do with nerves.

Knowing enough time had passed, she turned around and glanced at the stick on the counter and her knees buckled at what she saw. Apparently no matter how much you prepared yourself, finding out you were pregnant by a man who didn't want forever with you was a punch of gut-wrenching reality.

She lowered herself onto the closed toilet seat and put her head in her hands. "Okay, okay, think," she said to herself.

First, she had to testify. She had to put that mess behind her. Austin would protect her and she'd get through that this week. Then, before he brought Bailey home, she'd tell him that she was pregnant.

She had to pull in deep breaths at the reminder.

She wouldn't trap him. He didn't want a future with her and she didn't want him because he felt obligated. He'd been in that situation once before and had been cornered into marriage. She wouldn't hide the truth from him but she wouldn't accept him marrying her out of guilt, either.

She could raise this baby by herself. How, she didn't quite know the details yet. But plenty of women managed and she'd do the same thing. Just not as Bailey's nanny. The thought of leaving the little girl hurt, but there was no way she could stay on. And there was every chance Austin wouldn't want her to.

She had a healthy savings account thanks to room and board being part of any previous employment, and she'd be able to rent an apartment somewhere. Maybe the city, where she could get a job within walking or subway distance and not need a car.

See? She could do this. She just had to survive this week of the trial and then telling Austin she was pregnant with his baby.

SOMETHING WAS UP with Mia and damned if Austin could figure it out. Things were bad before they'd gone to Dan's, but afterwards, she'd totally withdrawn into herself. To his knowledge, nothing had happened there that would upset her except that she'd obviously gotten sick. He was damned sure going to make certain she saw a doctor once she finished testifying, because he was beginning to be concerned.

He planned to bring his daughter home by Friday, once Mia's testimony was over and there was nothing her ex-employer could gain by going after her. The damage would be done by then. But he missed her like crazy and wanted to take her for pizza and ice cream tonight. He'd also thought Mia would enjoy getting out of the house, but she'd insisted on staying at home.

"You need time alone with Bailey," she'd said.

"But Bailey wants to see you, too."

A wistful smile had pulled at her lips. "I'd like that, too. But I think it's more important for you to have father-daughter bonding time."

Which was why he sat across from his daughter at an old-fashioned pizza parlor. His parents had joined them and they'd ordered two pizzas, one plain and one with pepperoni.

"Did Grandma tell you I want a fish?" Bailey asked after she'd swallowed a bite of her food.

Austin nearly choked on his pizza. "No, Grandma didn't mention it."

His mother grinned. "She actually wants a puppy but I managed to talk her down to a fish," she said, her eyes glittering with mischief.

Austin supposed he was lucky his mom hadn't encouraged his daughter's desire for a dog… although he really was giving it thought. He just wouldn't mention it to Bailey in case he decided against it.

Bailey pushed herself up on her knees on the booth bench. "Yeah, I wanted a dog, Daddy. But Grandma said you're too busy working. But I told her Mia takes such good care of me, she could take care of the dog, too."

As if Mia needed another thing to care for. "I think we'd have to talk to Mia about any pet you get, honey."

"Does that mean maybe a dog? Can we go to a puppy store? Please?" Bailey squeezed her hands together like she was praying.

Austin blinked, uncertain how they'd gone from fish back to puppy in the blink of an eye. "First of all, if we did ever get a dog, we'd adopt one."

"Connor in my class is adopted," Bailey said. "His mommy said he's extra-special because she picked him. I think I'm extra special because you're my daddy." She picked up her pizza and took a large bite, smearing grease across her cheeks and not caring.

He wiped her face with a huge lump in his throat because this child meant so damned much to him. It didn't matter to him how he'd had her, it only mattered that he did.

"You are extra-special, Bailey Button." He met his father's, then mother's gaze. Both their eyes were filling, too. "Okay, should we take the leftovers home?" he asked.

"Yeah. Would you give some to Mia?" Bailey asked.

"Sure thing."

"How is Mia?" his mother asked. "I was hoping she'd come for dinner."

He frowned at the question because he really didn't know how Mia was. "She's... she hasn't been herself. She was sick and it's lingered. I think it's got her all out of sorts."

"Maybe you should talk to her and find out what's going on," his mother suggested.

"I asked if she's okay. Beyond that, there isn't much I can do. I'm sure she has a lot on her mind, what with testifying this week."

"Hmm. Well, I hope she feels better."

"Me, too."

And it wasn't like there was anything more he could do for her, Austin thought, because Mia certainly wasn't communicating with him.

Chapter Eleven

"I'M NERVOUS," MIA admitted as Austin pulled the car into a parking lot in Manhattan for her trial prep with the district attorney. "I mean, not nervous for the prep but for the trial on Friday, which is ridiculous considering I've done this before."

"It's normal to be worked up. First of all, this guy has been trying to scare you away from testifying. And second, it's nerve-racking not knowing what the defense is going to ask you. The good news is, it'll all be over soon." He placed his hand on hers, and to his surprise, she didn't pull back.

Her skin was soft and his dick noticed. Of course it did. It was the first time he'd really touched her since he'd carried her up to his bed.

Taken care of her.

Fallen asleep beside her.

Woken up holding her, her lithe, warm body curled back into his.

Since life had felt right and good if only she hadn't been sick. And she'd been sick for a while now. A niggling thought suddenly prickled at his brain.

No. They'd used protection.

But maybe it hadn't worked?

One thing he knew for sure, if she was pregnant, unlike Kayla, Mia hadn't arranged for it to happen.

How had he not recognized the possibility before? It wasn't the flu, no fever, no cough, chills, congestion. And the longer it went on, the less likely it was a stomach bug.

Hell, it had been right in front of him this whole time and he'd been blind. Because Kayla had had a textbook perfect pregnancy, no morning sickness at all.

Mia could be pregnant.

Fuck.

But instead of panic, he felt an overwhelming sense of rightness settle over him, making him wonder, what the hell had he been fighting so damned hard against?

She was his perfect complement in all ways. An out-of-the-blue realization? Maybe. Or maybe not. Maybe it had been floating around in the back of his mind for a long time now but he'd taken his time coming to the right place because she'd been there all along.

He'd been an ass, letting things go on as they'd been, Mia always there in his life but not where she should be. In his bed. In his heart.

He loved her.

He blinked. Glanced at her delicate profile, the serious expression on her face an indicator of the way she'd withdrawn from him because he'd let her.

"Austin? I asked if you're ready to get out of the car," she said, concern in her voice.

He blinked. "Yeah." He wasn't. Inside he was trembling.

He wanted nothing more than to take her into his arms and put her out of her misery. Whether she knew, suspected, or not, she needed him. But there was something she had to get through first and it needed her focus. However, when this mess that was screwing with her life ended, they were going to have a serious talk about their future.

Because her being *around* wasn't enough for him. Not when she'd become as essential to him as breathing.

He climbed out and strode around to her side, helping her stand. "Are you feeling okay?" he asked. She'd seemed fine this morning but he had the sense she was hiding as much as she could from him... and now he understood why.

"Yes. Better today," she said, ducking her head,

not meeting his gaze.

She obviously didn't want him to know. Because he'd made it clear he didn't want to start over with marriage, a family. He damned himself for being so clueless.

"You ready to do this?" he asked.

She nodded. "I don't think I'll be in with Kate for long. An hour, tops."

"I'll be waiting when you get out. I'm not leaving you alone."

"I appreciate that."

He dealt with the parking lot attendant and led Mia out to the street. On the walk to the office, he kept an eye on everything going on around him. The city was busy, people rushing to work on a normal morning, but he had an arm around Mia, holding her close, ready to protect her if need be.

They approached the building, which had five steps up and a set of double doors through which to enter. Before they reached the first step, Mia looked down and her sunglasses fell from her head to the ground.

She paused, bending down to retrieve them at the same time Austin caught sight of a man with a gun. Everything happened at once. The man fired as Austin shoved her to the ground, doing his best to take the brunt of the fall even as he kept her beneath the protection of his body.

Mia screamed. People around them shouted, in a panic. And Austin had to let the shooter go to concentrate on Mia.

He turned her onto her back. "Hey, baby." He looked into her eyes, his heart pounding with the thought that he could have lost her. "Are you okay?"

She shook her head and he glanced down, seeing flecks of blood staining through her clothes. Jesus Christ, she'd been shot. Nausea rushed through him.

He pulled her into his arms, covering her body with his own. "Fuck." Anger and fury pulsed inside him, both at himself and the bastard who'd been so brazen as to shoot in a crowd.

He glanced around but they were surrounded by onlookers and the assailant was long gone. "Someone call 911!" he shouted to the people around them, then refocused on Mia. "I'll get you out of here, just hang on. I've got you."

Tears pooled in her eyes. "I'm fine. My shoulder burns but… I'm okay," she said, as if he were the one who needed reassuring. "But—"

"Give me a second." He ripped off his jacket and pressed it against the wound, applying pressure.

She winced at the pain.

"I'm sorry but I have to staunch the bleeding."

"Ambulance is on its way," someone yelled to him.

He breathed out a harsh breath.

Suddenly Mia grabbed his arm with her good hand. "Austin, I'm scared."

He leaned closer, his lips near her cheek. "It's going to be okay."

"But…" She drew a shuddering breath, her gaze hesitant. "I'm pregnant. What about the baby?"

The sound of sirens blared and relief flooded him. She said it was her shoulder that burned but until he knew if that bullet exited and didn't hit anything vital, he wouldn't breathe.

He sucked in a shallow breath, possibility suddenly becoming definite. In the chaos of her getting shot, he'd forgotten his earlier thoughts about her possibly having his baby.

"I know you are," he said with a soft smile. "I figured it out, but right now we're going to focus on you, and when the ambulance gets here, we'll fill them in."

Her eyes opened wide at his admission. "You know?"

"I just figured it out as we pulled into the garage." He pushed harder on the jacket as the ambulance pulled up to the curb.

Paramedics ran out and pushed Austin aside. He knew the drill but it still rankled. "She's pregnant," he informed them. "Make sure they're both okay."

"We're on it. Just stay back," a female said.

Austin couldn't see over their backs or shoulders and he was in a panic of his own. Finally, they put her on a stretcher and he ran up beside her, grasping her hand.

"Sir, you can't—"

"I'm her fiancé. I'm coming with her," he said in his sternest, most insistent voice.

Mia's eyes grew wide in her now pale face.

Ignoring her shock, he pushed past the paramedics and joined her in the back of the ambulance.

★ ★ ★

MIA LAY ON a bed in the emergency room, her shoulder burning, the pain agonizing, but she was fortunate the bullet had only grazed her. The amount of blood after the shooting had been deceiving as far as the damage done. They'd given her a painkiller, assuring her it was safe for the baby in the early stages of pregnancy, and considering the level of pain she was in, she decided not to argue. She'd take it to get over the initial pain and cut back as soon as possible.

Now she had to face Austin. The fact that they hadn't let him back with her while they worked on her shoulder was a blessing because she didn't want to deal with the baby talk on top of everything else going on. But now she was alone, it was quiet, and she'd have to deal with the fact of her pregnancy and her future.

The sweet nurse who'd been by her side through the worst of the cleaning of the wound had gone out to get her fiancé, as he'd called himself to the paramedics. Not that she blamed him. The label enabled him to stay by her side and she appreciated not being alone and afraid at the same time.

"Hello?" Austin pushed aside the curtain. "Is it okay if I come in?"

"Sure."

He stepped into the small cubicle in which she'd been placed. One look at him and she knew he wasn't doing well. He'd taken off his jacket to staunch her blood loss and now wore a rumpled white shirt, sleeves haphazardly rolled up. His hair stood on end as if he'd been running his fingers through it over and over again. He was pale, his eyes glazed, and her heart squeezed tight in her chest.

She hadn't meant to put him through something so traumatic, and though she understood this was his job, even she had to admit he'd been affected by today's events.

"Hey." He came up to her bed and gripped the metal side rail.

"Hey."

Unable to help herself, she reached out and placed her hand over his. "I'm okay," she reassured him. "The bullet grazed my shoulder. It didn't penetrate or do any major damage."

"Because you dropped your glasses. Otherwise you would have taken a direct hit somewhere more vital. I wish I'd been on your other side," he said, teeth clenched, his frustration and anger with himself obvious.

"You couldn't have guessed where he'd be."

Austin nodded, his jaw tight, as if he really did know that, he just hated the fact that she'd been hurt.

Silence followed for a few minutes and he finally spoke. "Are we going to talk about it?" he asked.

She glanced down at her still-flat stomach. "We should." She ran her tongue over her dry lips. "I was going to tell you right after the trial."

He inclined his head. "I believe you. I just can't really wrap my head around the fact that you're pregnant. I mean, we used protection, no holes in the condoms," he said wryly.

"It happens." She still looked down, needing to gather herself as she said what she'd planned to say next. "Austin…"

"Yeah?"

"I don't expect anything from you."

"Mia," he said, a definite warning in his tone.

She shook her head. "No. Let me finish."

He waved a dismissive hand. "Go ahead."

She swallowed hard. "I know this happened to you

before."

A low growl escaped him but she forged on. "You got a woman pregnant and it wasn't planned and you felt obligated to marry her and try to create a family for Bailey's sake. And I admire and respect that about you, I really do. But I want you to know, I've heard you loud and clear."

She looked up in time to see him narrow his gaze. "You heard what?"

"I heard you when you told me you didn't want anything serious, and more importantly, I heard you tell Ben you've done the family thing once and you weren't going to do it again." She ran her tongue over her lips. "I wasn't eavesdropping. I was waiting for the bathroom at Dan's," she said quietly. "And I respect you too much to ever put you in that position again."

"Are you finished?" he asked, his tone low and brittle.

"No," she said, her head buzzing, dizziness and emotional pain assaulting her. "There's one more thing. I won't stop you from having whatever relationship you want with our child." She met his gaze. "Now I'm finished."

"Good. Because you have everything wrong."

She blinked up at him. The fluorescent lights from above her head were harsh and she glanced down. "I don't know what you mean."

She couldn't imagine how she'd been mistaken in any of this.

He jiggled the bed rail until he lowered it and sat on the bed beside her. He picked up her hand, and her heart rate spiked at the feel of his more calloused fingers entwined with hers.

"Let's start with Kayla. She tricked me into marriage, and yes, I married her because she was pregnant, but here's the difference between you and my ex-wife." His grip tightened around hers. "I love *you*."

She blinked and tears fell from her eyes. It was everything she wanted to hear, and she understood that, if they were going to have any kind of future, she needed to start trusting in things she'd never quite let herself believe in. She needed to trust in him.

She was overwhelmed by his words and the events of the day as she spoke. "Austin, I—"

"Shh." He leaned over and kissed her cheek. "You've had a rough day, a shock to your body, and now this. I know you want to believe me and you're afraid. You might even think I'm saying I love you because you're pregnant, but when you think about things, think about this. I married Kayla, yes, but I never told her I loved her."

Her eyes opened wide as the meaning and import of his words sunk in.

"Ms. Atwood?" A nurse pushed the curtain aside.

"The police want to talk to you. We have to report all gunshots, you understand."

She wanted to decline the visit, to focus on Austin and all the new feelings floating around inside her. Of course, the floating could be the painkillers, but the high caused by his words? Not so much.

"You can send them in," she said, shooting Austin a regret-filled glance.

"Don't worry. I'm not going anywhere," he promised, his hand still in hers.

And though she hadn't processed what his proclamation really meant for them, the baby, or her future, she squeezed his fingers tighter as she prepared to deal with the police. At least now, her heart was light and her entire body filled with hope.

★   ★   ★

AUSTIN SAT BY Mia's side, refusing to leave when she spoke to the police. He gripped her tighter when she repeated the details of the shooting. The entire incident had been running on replay in his head ever since. They took his statement, as well, and he knew she still had to talk to the district attorney, but finally the officer left, walking through the curtain, and they were alone until the doctor signed off on Mia's release.

"Hey," he said, treating her to a concerned half smile. "Are you okay?"

Her skin was pale, eyes half-mast.

"I'm hanging in there. How about you?"

"The same." He ran his thumb over the smooth skin of her hand. "I want you to know something else. I realize you don't come from a family where love is abundant, and because of that, your ability to trust is somewhat compromised."

She studied him, obviously invested in what he was saying.

"I also realize I didn't help my case by telling you, and repeating, that I didn't want marriage or a future with you."

She blinked and a tear leaked down her cheek. He caught it with his hand.

"I'd kick my own ass if I could—for being so shortsighted and for hurting you. But since I can't, I'm just going to have to do my best to convince you that I was wrong. I was afraid to believe in you. In us. And I hope you won't follow my example of running away from what could be, what is the best thing to ever happen to us."

He grasped her other hand, too, and held both up to his chest. "I love you, Mia. And I want to spend every day I have left showing you how much. The baby is icing on an already spectacular cake."

She laughed. "So now I'm a cake."

"You're sweet enough."

She rolled her eyes at his silly joke before sobering. "You're right, you know. Everything you said about my past, my fears, you nailed it all. And a part of me really wants to run away because it's easier than believing everything I ever wanted is within my grasp."

"And what is it you want?" He held his breath as she spoke, hoping with everything in him they desired the same things and she was brave enough to go after them.

"You. Bailey. A family." She visibly swallowed hard. "When we first got together, I knew it was dangerous for me because you represented all the things that could make my life complete. The things I didn't have growing up. Parents who loved each other and their children. But you didn't want that. Only I did."

He remained silent even though he wanted to pull her into his arms, giving her the same chance to speak that she'd given him. But he was sorry he'd put her through the pain of wanting, longing, when he should have had his eyes opened sooner.

"But now you're saying you've changed your mind. And I can believe you… or not."

"I'm hoping you will," he said, unable to remain quiet any longer.

"I do," she whispered. "Because I love you, too."

Her affirmation was all he needed. Careful to protect her shoulder, he leaned into her, pressing his lips to hers. With a soft moan of acceptance, she slid her tongue over his and he slipped his inside her waiting mouth.

The kiss couldn't go further despite the hard bulge growing behind his jeans, even if he did have the urge to crawl into the bed with her, align his body with hers, and lose himself in her warmth and heat.

"Knock knock!" A nurse said, pushing the curtain aside and letting herself into the small cubicle. "Sorry to interrupt you lovebirds but I have your discharge papers."

Austin grinned, aware of Mia blushing beside him. "My fiancée would be happy to sign your papers."

"Wait, what? We didn't... You didn't ask—" Mia stuttered over her words.

"Didn't I say that I love you and I want to spend every day I have left showing you how much?" he asked, aware they had an amused and rapt audience in the nurse.

Mia blinked. "You did. But—"

"What did you think I meant?"

She grinned at him. "You silly man. I would think you'd ask me if you meant you wanted to marry me!"

"Will you marry me?" he asked, his gaze never leaving hers.

"Yes."

"Good. Ring and proper proposal to follow. I just didn't want to leave here without being one hundred percent clear on where we stood." He rose to his feet, never letting go of her hand.

The nurse sighed. "Sometimes we have a good day. And today was definitely one of those. How romantic," she murmured.

Austin was pretty damned pleased himself.

"Now can we go over your discharge instructions?" the nurse asked, back to business.

THE NEXT FEW days passed in a blur, the focus not on their personal lives but on Mia's testimony, something Austin was determined to see her through. The district attorney came to the house the day after the shooting and went over court prep with Mia. She'd also assured them they now had police officers watching the house and sticking by Mia's side through the trial and until Parker Alexander was back in jail, where he belonged.

Austin spoke to the DA and all agreed Parker's agenda had been to prevent Mia, the key witness against him, from testifying. Once that was over, he'd turn his focus elsewhere. Revenge wasn't his MO. Self-preservation was. When Mia's testimony was finished and the verdict was in, she would be safe. And she'd have him by her side to make her security a certainty.

She was set to testify only two days after the shooting, and she insisted on showing up on time. She wanted the trial over with and he didn't blame her. As long as she felt physically capable, he would support her all the way.

The bad news was that Austin wasn't sleeping, because when he shut his eyes, he saw Mia covered in blood, remembered holding his jacket on her shoulder to stop the flow. The good news was that he now had her by his side, in his bed. He took care of her day and night, catering to her shoulder and the pain she was in and repeating how much he loved her.

The day of her testimony, it went like clockwork. She walked through the city streets and entered the courtroom surrounded by protection on all sides.

Her words were damning, her demeanor calm, her voice strong as she testified. Not even the gunshot or the bandage covering her arm kept her from doing the right thing, and Austin was so damned proud of her.

Their lives as a family could soon begin.

AFTER THE TRIAL testimony ended and Mia walked out of the courtroom, Parker's angry eyes on her as she went, she felt as if a huge weight had been lifted off her shoulders. She refused to be afraid now that it was over. Parker should go back to jail and he no longer had a reason to want her out of the way. She'd done her duty.

An hour later, they returned to the house. Austin's parents' car was parked in the driveway.

"Bailey's home?" she asked, excited.

"I thought it was time. But don't worry. You're still healing and you don't need to take care of her," Austin said.

"What? Of course I want to take care of her. I'll do what I can with this arm. They want me to keep it immobilized. But I don't want to scare her, either. So what's our story? What happened to me?"

He studied her, a soft smile on his face.

"What?" she asked, uncomfortable under his intense scrutiny.

"You worry more about Bailey than yourself. It's one of the things I love about you."

Her heart fluttered at his words and she wondered if she'd ever get used to hearing it. She hoped not.

"If she asks, we'll tell her you fell. She won't know the difference."

No sooner had they walked into the house from the garage than Bailey came running. "Daddy! Mia! I'm home!" she yelled, crashing into Austin's legs.

"Hey!" He swung her into his arms, one eye on Mia.

She smiled, reassuring him she was fine.

"Oh, Mia!" His mother rushed up to them. "I've been so worried about you," she said, lowering her voice at the end so Bailey wouldn't catch her concern.

"Thank you but I'm fine. I promise."

Sarah squeezed her hands. "You're a strong, brave woman."

Tears sprung to Mia's eyes. If this was what she had to look forward to in her life, wonderful people caring about her, she was even luckier than she had thought.

"Hey, everyone, let's go sit. Mia and I have something to tell you," Austin said.

They'd talked about filling Bailey in on their engagement and the fact that she would be having a baby brother or sister, but they hadn't said when. Mia was coming to realize that Austin was impatient when it came to things that he wanted.

They settled into the sofa in the family room, Mia and Austin on one corner of the sofa, his parents on the other, a pleased, hopeful look on Sarah's face.

"Come up here, baby." Austin patted his thighs and Bailey came and sat on his lap. "So here's the thing. You know how much you love Mia?" He looked at his daughter, love in his expressive brown eyes.

"So much," Bailey said, causing Mia's breath to catch.

"Well, Daddy loves Mia, too." He reached out and

grasped Mia's hand, pulling her close.

His mother gasped and his father chuckled with pleasure at his wife's reaction, while Mia sat happy and overwhelmed by the emotions both filling and surrounding her.

"So Mia and I are going to get married," he went on, talking to his daughter, but now his mother started to cry happy tears.

"Is that okay with you?" Mia asked the little girl. "Because more than anything, we want you to be happy."

Bailey glanced at her through curious eyes. "Does this mean you're my mommy?"

Mia wasn't sure what to say. Once again, hope filled her as she deferred the answer to Austin.

"Is that what you want?" he asked.

Bailey wrinkled her little nose in thought and Mia continued to hold her breath.

"Well, duh!" she finally said. "I told you I wanted a mommy. And now I get my pick in mommies!" She dove forward and threw her arms around Mia's neck.

Ignoring the stabbing pain in her shoulder, Mia hugged the little girl back. "I love that you're my first baby girl," she said, her voice thick.

Austin carefully pried Bailey off Mia's injured arm. "I guess this means now that things have settled down, I can leave the house and buy a ring."

"Oh, Austin. Didn't I raise you better? You should have had that thing on you when you proposed," his father muttered.

Mia laughed. Little did they know, she didn't need the ring. All she needed were the people in this room and now part of her family.

Especially the man who'd changed her life and gave her so much more than anything he could buy her. He gave her love.

Thank you for reading TEMPT ME. I hope you enjoyed Austin and Mia's story! I would appreciate it if you would help others enjoy this book by leaving a review at your preferred e-tailer.

Keep up with me by joining my newsletter: www.carlyphillips.com/newsletter-sign-up

Up next: A new set of siblings and family fun and drama! Fall in love with the Wards beginning with FEARLESS coming March 20, 2018.
Please PREORDER FEARLESS today.

Read an excerpt of Fearless:

FEARLESS

Fall in love with the Wards…

Mechanic and garage owner, Kane Harmon is used to the wealthy beautiful women visiting his beach town. He doesn't get involved because he knows most females would merely be slumming for the summer.

Except Hayley Ward isn't just passing through. She lives a solitary life in a bungalow on the beach. A woman tormented by her past, distant from her wealthy family, different from Kane's usual fare of town girls who know his M.O. – Don't expect more than he's willing to give.

Kane rescues Hayley and her broken down car from the side of the road and instantly he's hooked. She says she's not interested in him. He knows she lies. And he makes it his mission to bring her back to life, to return her emotionally to her family. To show her the colors around her were as vibrant as the ones she puts on her canvas.

Until past meets present and Kane's life threatens all the progress they've made. Then it's Hayley's turn to step up and stand up for the relationship and life she's finally coming to believe she deserves.

Fearless

Excerpt

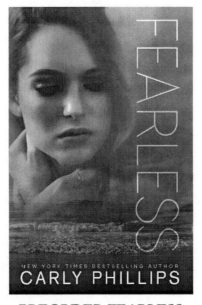

PREORDER FEARLESS

Fearless Photo and cover: Sara Eirew

Chapter One

"KANE! PICK UP on Route 5. Lady needs a tow," Kane Harmon's father, Joe, called out from the office in Harmon's Garage.

Kane wiped his greasy hands on a rag and pushed himself out from beneath the jacked-up car he'd been working on. He rose to his feet and glanced around the empty shop, taking stock of his situation. Jackson Traynor, who usually handled the runs with the tow was out. He'd gone to the city to pick up an emergency part, meaning Kane and his dad were the only ones here. Joe, who Kane had no desire to leave by himself.

Temptation was always too great for Kane's father. If he could pocket something to pawn, trade or sell for extra cash, he'd do it to fuel his gambling addiction. Unfortunately, Kane couldn't send his dad out on the run because the older man was no longer allowed to drive. Too many accidents and he'd had his license revoked.

But Kane wasn't going to leave a woman stranded on the highway, so he'd have to go take care of the tow himself. He headed for the office and found his father sitting behind the desk, writing on a scrap pad. Kane hoped it wasn't notes on horses or ball games.

"Hey," Kane said, striding around to the back of the desk, coming up behind his father. "I'm going to go do the pick up since Jackson's out." While he spoke, he pulled a key out of his pocket and opened the cash drawer, removing the bills that were in there.

At a glance, there were hundreds, fifties and smaller bills separated in the till. He didn't leave anything behind to provide his father the least little bit of temptation.

"You've got to be shitting me." His father's eyes were on the money Kane shoved into his front pockets. "You don't trust me," he said, sullenly.

"No, dad, I don't. Why should I?"

There'd been holiday money he'd gambled away when they were kids and when things were bad his dad's motto was, *if it wasn't nailed down, it's fair game.* Kane didn't feel the least bit guilty doing what he had to do to make sure he could provide for the family when his father couldn't. Joe wouldn't steal while Kane was in the shop. Kane knew that. It was only when nobody was around to see or answer to, that the demon on his shoulder got the best of him and temptation took over.

His dad muttered something under his breath, undecipherable but obviously mean, and Kane chose to ignore him.

"I shouldn't be gone long. Hold down the fort?" Kane asked.

"Oh. You'll trust me to talk to customers?" Sarcasm dripped from his dad's words. "Last time I looked it was my name on the signage," he muttered.

And last time Kane checked, he was the one running the business. True, the building was in his father's name, but the old man wouldn't budge on adding Kane or his siblings to the deed. The only salvation was the fact that Joe knew his limitations. He'd turned the business over to Kane when he turned twenty-two, after a bad run with some loan sharks. Kane stepped in and paid off the debt and in exchange, the business was in Kane's name. Just not the land. Kane wanted it divided between the three siblings but his father's pride demanded he hold onto it until he passed on. Which, thank God, didn't look like it would be any time soon.

His father drove Kane mad but he loved his old man. Joe raised them since his mom died from Ovarian cancer when Kane had been fifteen and had done the best he could with the limited skill set he had. His heart was in the right place even if his vices weren't.

Kane palmed the truck keys in his hands. "Don't forget Nicky's coming by after school," he reminded his dad.

His sister Joy's seven-year-old son spent afternoons at the garage with his uncle and grandfather while his mom worked. With Nicky's father out of his life – and good riddance – it was important for Nicky to spend time with the men in his family. Not to mention it freed his sister up to work and not worry about her kid after school. And Kane liked having his nephew around. Even if he was under a car, Nicky did his homework in the office and chatted up his grandpa. It was good.

Kane stepped into the blazing, late afternoon sunshine, appreciating the summer heat on his face. Once he was outside, he forgot about the aggravation with his dad and instead appreciated the fresh air after being cooped under a car for the better part of the day.

He popped his aviators on his face and climbed into the flatbed, starting up the engine. He drove out of town and onto the highway, music blasting on the radio, catching sight of the gleaming, what looked like new, bright red Ford SUV on the side of the road.

The influx of summer visitors usually meant expensive foreign cars littering the side of the main street and taking up the prime parking near the beach. This little beauty didn't strike him as one of those but he didn't recognize it as one of his regulars, either.

He pulled in behind the SUV onto the shoulder of the road and parked. Hopping out, he strode to the front of his vehicle and caught sight of a woman in a flirty dress bent over the open hatch, as she draped what looked like a sheet over something in the far back.

He shoved his hands into the front pocket of his jeans and looked his fill of the sweet ass aimed in the air and long legs leaning against the edge of the back, his dick perking up and taking notice.

Before he could make his presence known, though she had to have heard his truck's arrival, she turned around and met his gaze.

Recognition slammed into him, raw and real. "Halley Ward," he muttered. "Well, I'll be damned." The girl he knew not at all but had protected from bullying back in high school stood before him, all grown up.

"Hi, Kane," she said softly, shading her eyes from the sun with her hands. Eyes he knew were a light blue.

She'd been quiet and withdrawn back then, head almost always hidden inside a hooded sweatshirt, only her two long braids hanging out from her protective armor. But he knew her story.

Everyone did.

Rescued from foster care at fifteen by her aunt, Halley never seemed to adjust to life back home with her wealthy family. She didn't reach out to other girls or make friends at school or in town. Or maybe they didn't welcome her. He hadn't been sure. He'd only known that at the time, he had recently lost his mom and pulled back from the world, so he recognized that same sense of sadness and loss in Halley and had stepped in when the kids gave her a rough time. They'd never talked or bonded but he knew she appreciated his efforts. Could tell by the lingering, sad but grateful looks she passed him in the hall that his actions meant something to her.

Despite living in the same town, he hadn't seen her in years. She was more solitary than he was and she didn't hang out at the The Dive, the main bar in town on Friday or Saturday nights. Had he wondered about her through the years? Sure. But life went on.

"So. Dead SUV?" he asked, gesturing to her ride.

"Dead *new* SUV," she said, sounding pissed off. "What kind of new car just… dies?" She braced her hands on her slender hips and frowned at her vehicle.

He shrugged. "Won't know until I get jacked it up and take a look." He met her gaze. "How've you been?" he asked.

"Good." She toyed with a strand of hair.

With the sun streaming down, her took in those

brown locks with sun kissed streaks of blonde closer to the ends that hung just past her shoulders. And he immediately noticed that the face she hid as a kid was all the more striking now.

Seriously.

She was fucking beautiful. And still fragile at least in appearance, her skin like porcelain, her features delicate with a hint of freckles over the bridge of her nose. And there was still that hint of sadness that fell over her features, there whether she was aware of it or not.

"You?" she asked. "How are you doing? Still working at the garage, I see?"

He'd had a job there from the time he was a kid, hanging out from a young age, just as Nicky did now.

Kane nodded. "I run the place," he wasn't sure why he felt compelled to let her know.

"That's good." She ran her hands up and down her arms.

"Hey, let me get your truck on the flatbed and we'll go back to the garage. I'll take a quick look and see if I can tell you what we're dealing with."

"Thanks."

"You're welcome to hang out in the front of the cab while I work," he said.

She smiled. "And thanks again." She spun on her low-heeled sandals and her floral dress, which clung to her curves, spun out around her thighs.

Flirty. Cute. Sexy as fuck.

He did his thing and soon they were on their way back to the garage. "So what's covered in the back of your truck?" he asked, having seen the sheet for himself.

"Paintings. I paint. My work is in the gallery in town. I was taking a few pieces over when my car died and I didn't want the sun beating down and fading them."

"Wow. That's cool. I'll have to stop by the place and see your work." He was impressed with that little bit of knowledge about her.

His hands on the wheel, he glanced over. A blush stained her cheeks. "I'm not sure my work is your style."

"Doesn't mean I don't want to see it anyway. Besides, how would you know what my style is?"

"You're right. I don't," she murmured. She curled her hands around her purse on her lap and he refocused on the road.

"Maybe we could change that." Now where had that suggestion come from?

Her gaze swung to his. Startled. "What are you saying"

"Go out with me some time." No, he hadn't planned it but Halley Ward intrigued him. She always had.

"I don't date." That surprised him... but it shouldn't, now that he gave it thought.

It wasn't like he saw her out and about anyway and she did like to keep to herself. But not to even date? What was that all about?

"Then call it two old friends catching up," he said, now even more determined to find out.

He glanced over to find her lips twitching in amusement she was obviously trying not to show. She might not want to be interested in going out with him... but she was.

"We weren't friends," she reminded him gently.

"Do friends stand up for each other?" he asked.

She nodded. "They do."

"Then I'd consider us friends." He looked at her and winked. "Just think about it," he said as he pulled into the garage lot.

Because she intrigued him. Maybe it was fate that her car broke down and he'd been the one to answer the call, bringing them together again after all these years. They were adults now and he wanted to get to know what lay behind those blue eyes, what secrets she held. Because he sensed, then and now, that her layers ran deep.

PREORDER FEARLESS

Keep up with Carly and her upcoming books:

Website:
www.carlyphillips.com

Sign up for Carly's Newsletter:
www.carlyphillips.com/newsletter-sign-up

Carly on Facebook:
www.facebook.com/CarlyPhillipsFanPage

Carly on Twitter:
www.twitter.com/carlyphillips

Hang out at Carly's Corner! (Hot guys & giveaways!)
smarturl.it/CarlysCornerFB

About the Author

Carly Phillips is the *N.Y. Times* and *USA Today* Bestselling Author of over 50 sexy contemporary romance novels featuring hot men, strong women and the emotionally compelling stories her readers have come to expect and love. Carly's career spans over a decade and a half with various New York publishing houses, and she is now an Indie author who runs her own business and loves every exciting minute of her publishing journey. Carly is happily married to her college sweetheart, the mother of two nearly adult daughters and three crazy dogs (two wheaten terriers and one mutant Havanese) who star on her Facebook Fan Page and website. Carly loves social media and is always around to interact with her readers. You can find out more about Carly at www.carlyphillips.com.